*pretty*TOUGH

*pretty*TOUGH

a novel by

liz tigelaar

razOr
bill

PrettyTOUGH

RAZORBILL

Published by the Penguin Group
Penguin Young Readers Group
345 Hudson Street, New York, New York 10014, U.S.A.
Penguin Group (USA) Inc., 375 Hudson Street, New York, New York 10014, U.S.A.
Penguin Group (Canada), 90 Eglinton Avenue East, Suite 700, Toronto, Ontario,
Canada M4P 2Y3 (a division of Pearson Penguin Canada Inc.)
Penguin Books Ltd, 80 Strand, London WC2R 0RL, England
Penguin Ireland, 25 St Stephen's Green, Dublin 2, Ireland
(a division of Penguin Books Ltd)
Penguin Group (Australia), 250 Camberwell Road, Camberwell,
Victoria 3124, Australia (a division of Pearson Australia Group Pty Ltd)
Penguin Books India Pvt Ltd, 11 Community Centre, Panchsheel Park,
New Delhi – 110 017, India
Penguin Group (NZ), Cnr Airborne and Rosedale Roads, Albany,
Auckland 1310, New Zealand (a division of Pearson New Zealand Ltd)
Penguin Books (South Africa) (Pty) Ltd, 24 Sturdee Avenue, Rosebank,
Johannesburg 2196, South Africa

Penguin Books Ltd, Registered Offices: 80 Strand, London WC2R 0RL, England

10 9 8 7 6 5

Library of Congress Cataloging-in-Publication Data

Tigelaar, Liz.
PrettyTough / by Liz Tigelaar.
    p. cm.
Summary: Two feuding sisters from Malibu, California, take their rivalry to the soccer
field when both girls make the high school team.

ISBN-13: 978-1-59514-112-5
[1. Sisters—Fiction. 2. Sibling rivalry—Fiction. 3. Soccer—Fiction. 4. High schools—
Fiction. 5. Schools—Fiction. 6. Malibu (Calif.)—Fiction.] I. Title. II. Title: Pretty tough.

PZ7.T4525Pr 2007
[Fic]—dc22
                                                        2007001973

Printed in the United States of America

Pretty Tough is dedicated to every girl who has dared to dream — especially the original Pretty Tough girls Alex & Maddy.

one

For nearly twenty seconds, Charlie was convinced she was dead. Strangely, the thought didn't sound half bad. With her sophomore year of high school looming on the horizon, she'd already come to the conclusion that her first fifteen years on the planet were a bust. . . .

And yes, a lot of that had to do with her name.

Charlie Brown.

Obviously, her family had some sort of vendetta against her from the start. Obsessed with a *Peanuts* video at age two, Charlie's older sister, Krista, was the one who actually suggested the name.

In a fit of what must have been complete insanity, Charlie's parents actually thought it was a good idea.

Charlie scowled. *Who lets a two-year-old name a baby?*

Krista loved to lord over her the fact that she had named her almost as much as she loved pointing out that when Charlie was born, their dad had been hoping for a boy.

In junior high, when Charlie failed to develop boobs, Krista concluded that their dad got his wish.

Charlie couldn't decide what she hated most about her sister—her blond hair, her popular friends, her perfect boyfriend, or her distractingly loud phone voice. Luckily, Charlie didn't have to decide. She was content to hate it all.

From the day she was born, it seemed, Charlie Brown had started off on the wrong foot with the universe. And at this moment, having nose-dived off her surfboard into the sand below, she couldn't help but wonder if she was karmically jinxed. Unable to draw air into her lungs, she contemplated this thought as she lay facedown: Why not just surrender? If this was the end, then who was she to argue with destiny?

She felt the familiar tug of her leash on her ankle, her board being drawn toward the shore by the wave passing over her. Her fingers instinctively clawed the sand for support, for something.

Maybe this wasn't the end, Charlie thought, kicking toward the surface. Maybe there *were* things to live for. Like Friday night TV. If Charlie was going to die, it might as well be on Saturday, when there was nothing to watch.

Charlie opened her eyes as she broke through the waterline, scanning the horizon for any remainder of the wave that had been her undoing. Too late. It had vanished.

Another wave crashed over her, pushing her forward,

cementing the side of her face to the wet sand onshore. She hoped her bikini bottom was still intact and her butt wasn't hanging out for all of the Pacific Coast Highway to see.

Charlie could feel sand moving beneath her, and the momentum helped unstick her from her sandy crash site. In a burst of energy, she leapt up and was standing again. The only evidence of her monumental wipeout was a little bit of blood trickling down one side of her head.

She touched the wound with her fingertips and winced. Just a scrape—nothing catastrophic. But wasn't that usually the case? Wasn't it the little wounds that always hurt so badly?

She scanned her body for any other obvious injuries. Her mother had described her as lithe and athletic, but Charlie hated pretty much every inch of herself. An avid surfer and swimmer, she'd developed a lean, muscular frame—instead of boobs, like most girls.

Charlie's flatness made her feel freakish, especially when she compared herself to Krista—perfect Krista, who, naturally, had developed well and on schedule.

Charlie sighed at the undeniable truth—she didn't even fit in at her own house. Her mother, father, and sister made the perfect blond, blue-eyed family. With her brown hair and wider-than-she-would-like nose, Charlie was, without a doubt, the Ugly Duckling in a family full of swans.

She looked down and saw that her black nail polish was chipped. She resisted the urge to pick it off completely. Whatever. No one ever noticed her as a person. She supposed her nails were even more insignificant. She wondered why she'd even bothered painting them in the first place.

Charlie ran her fingers through her chin-length brown hair, streaked amber from the summer sun, and scanned the horizon. The waves were awesome—between eight and ten feet—and she'd been stoked for the great conditions, but all morning she'd had nothing but wipeouts. That last wave had left her pummeled.

Looking around, she was glad to see that she was alone. It wasn't surprising, really. These days she spent most of her time by herself. Krista was the social butterfly, always flitting off to parties, to the mall, to a date. . . .

Charlie gave a bitter chuckle. There was a time, she had to admit, when she actually admired her older sister— when she wanted to be just like her. But that was before last year. Before Krista let her down. . . .

Whatever. Charlie was over it. It didn't matter that she was alone. In fact, she preferred it that way.

After twenty minutes of contemplation and recovery, Charlie was ready to ride the surf again. Quitting on a humiliating low note was hardly an option, so she reached for the leash, velcroed it around her left ankle, and yanked the board back in a quick, familiar motion.

She grabbed the rails and ran out in the foamy surf. She had to catch a good wave before calling it a day. A little blood wasn't going to stop her.

She skidded belly-first onto her board. Her arms burned as she paddled out, the shores of Malibu growing distant behind her. She often wondered what would happen if she simply kept going, how long she could last out in the Pacific with nothing but her board.

Surely it would be easier than surviving one hour in school—in the presence of Regan Holder and her minions. Ugh. Regan.

A few smaller waves headed toward her. She stopped paddling and duck dived underneath them, passing smoothly and effortlessly through each one.

Sitting up on her board to get a better look, Charlie noticed a big swell on the horizon. A set was coming in. A class-A set. Her heart raced with anticipation. She saw the first wave. That was it. *Her* wave.

Quickly navigating her board around so that its nose was facing the beach, she felt the rumble of the wave bearing down.

Charlie reached her arms into the water. She dug deep, paddling furiously.

Faster, faster, she commanded herself.

There! She could feel the wave beneath her, lifting her up. This was the one!

Aggressive but smooth, fueled by adrenaline, Charlie

popped up, grabbing the board as she dropped into the wave. She pulled into the barrel, ducking low to make it through. The wave wrapped around her, enclosing her in the wall of water.

She shot through the tube—yes! Unable to conceal a smile, she rode the wave all the way into the beach and hopped off the board when she finally felt the sand beneath it.

She gave a little fist pump. She had just had the ride of her life. Or at least the day. Now, she thought, she could go home.

She jogged over to her bike, popped her head through her red Billabong hoodie, and gathered her stuff to leave. For a fleeting moment, she couldn't help but wish someone had been there to see her. . . .

"Excuse me? Are you Charlie?"

Charlie turned, surprised to find a young African American woman standing beside her. "Yeah?" Charlie asked cautiously.

"Charlie *Brown*," the woman stated. "That's you, right?"

Charlie bristled. "Yeah. And if you're going to ask 'Where's Linus?' or something, don't bother. I've heard it all before."

The woman smiled politely. "You looked great out there. Nice carve out of the barrel."

Charlie stopped short. This woman seemed to know what she was talking about. Who was she?

Charlie took in her outfit. Black-and-lime Puma chevron jacket over a faded Ramones shirt. Cargo shorts. Probably Abercrombie. Vans with no socks. She was maybe thirty years old. Charlie liked her style.

The woman extended her right hand. "I'm Martie."

"Uh-huh," Charlie answered hesitantly. Where was this going?

"You go to Beachwood, right? I subbed a couple of your classes last year."

Charlie didn't respond. She hated Beachwood with every fiber of her being. She hated going there, and she hated thinking about going there even more.

"I just got hired there permanently," Martie continued. "To coach."

"Good for you." Charlie shrugged.

"Oooh-kay." Martie gave a slight smirk. "Not the friendly type. Well, you might not know a lot about me, but I know *a lot* about you."

Charlie stared at her blankly.

"You were the star of your AYSO soccer league but quit a year and a half ago. You got first in girls' long board in the Sunshine Classic last year and third in short board. You've been featured as a 'teen to watch' in *Carve*. Your sister, Krista, is going to be a senior at Beachwood and—"

"Wait," Charlie interrupted. "Are you . . . stalking me?"

Martie laughed. "You call it stalking, I call it scouting. For Beachwood soccer."

Charlie scoffed. "My sister plays for Beachwood. This year? They're totally going to—" She caught herself, not wanting to be ruder than she already had a tendency to be.

"Suck?" Martie filled in. "I know. That's where I come in. And you, I hope."

Charlie slipped her shorts over her bikini bottoms. "I don't play soccer."

"But you did," Martie offered. "According to my research, for six years."

"Soccer is Krista's thing," Charlie said, struggling to put her surfboard on her bike's surf rack. "Well, that and admiring her own reflection."

Martie chuckled. "Maybe, but here's where I'm coming from. . . ." She grabbed Charlie's handlebars, holding the bike steady while Charlie secured the rack. "The school was recently given an endowment. A chunk of money to be used exclusively for girls' sports. To put Beachwood on the athletic map again. The first team we're revamping is the girls' soccer team because, well, soccer's kind of *my* thing, too. I'm looking for girls from all over LA, from South Central to the Valley to the Coast—not just soccer players necessarily, but tough athletes who are hungry to win. From the way you attacked that last wave, I'd say that's you."

"I'm not really a team player," Charlie said. She rolled her bike forward, hoping to end the conversation.

Martie put a hand on her arm, stopping her. "Wait. Just think about it, okay?" She smiled. "Maybe you've just never been on the right team."

Charlie looked at Martie through squinted eyes. Was this lady for real?

"You know, once upon a time? I went to Beachwood too. It's not an easy place to be." Martie gave Charlie's arm a squeeze. "But maybe this year, high school doesn't have to be as bad as you think."

At dinner that night, Charlie ate quietly as she always did, only half listening to Krista, who was, as usual, the center of her parents' attention. Outgoing, blond, and bursting with enthusiasm, Krista was always blabbering about *something*. More often than not, her dialogue centered around one topic: Brooks Sheridan.

"And then," Krista said to her parents, "Brooks told everyone she was going to Zuma. A second later, Buffi and Julie decided they wanted to go too. Can you *believe* it?"

Her voice was a little too loud, considering only three other people were at the table. Krista took a sip of her Diet Coke, straight out of the can. She drank only diet because she and Brooks were chronically watching their weight.

To the two of them, appearance was everything. One extra pound, one poor fashion choice meant the difference between acceptance—and being branded a loser.

Charlie scowled. She couldn't believe she had ever wanted to be like Krista.

Charlie glared as Krista droned on and on about her best friend. Not only were Krista and Brooks the most popular girls at Beachwood High, Brooks had actual *fans*. She'd been an actress since the age of five. Only three weeks ago, Brooks had finished shooting a movie that Charlie overheard her say was the next *Bend It Like Beckham*. Before that, she'd been in a martial arts movie where she had to train every day for five hours.

Brooks Sheridan—the perfect best friend for Charlie's perfect sister. It made Charlie want to vomit.

"What's so great about Brooks anyway?" she mumbled, moving her peas around on her plate to give the illusion that she had eaten most of them.

"What do you mean?" Krista asked, a frown twisting her glossy lips.

Charlie shrugged. "What's so great about her? I mean, you're just this lemming following her around, doing whatever she does. You don't even have your own identity—"

"I do plenty of things without Brooks," Krista said defensively.

"Yeah . . ." Charlie agreed. "But that's only because there isn't room in your Jetta for Brooks to make out with Cam too."

Cam and Krista had been dating for a little over a year. Tall, blond, and the captain of the football team, Cam simply had no earthly equal in Krista's mind. He was the cherry on top of her fairy-tale existence.

"Excuse me?" their mom asked, her perfectly arched eyebrows raised.

Emily Brown, a stay-at-home mom (who ironically was rarely home), was in her mid-forties. Although she was naturally beautiful, her looks had been enhanced by Charlie's dad, Bennett Brown, the renowned plastic surgeon. At least, "enhanced" was what Charlie's mom called it. Charlie called it straight-up fake.

"You heard me," Charlie said. "Krista shares everything with Brooks, right? Do you share Cam too?"

Krista's expression was a mix of confusion and disgust. "God. Why are you such a *freak?*"

"Girls," their dad ordered sternly. "Let's not do this at the dinner table."

Their mom stood up. "Who wants more mashed potatoes?" Their father rose from his seat and followed her into the kitchen.

Now that they were alone, Krista glared at Charlie. "What is wrong with you? Why do you always have to be such a beast?"

"Oh, I'm the beast?" Charlie snapped. "Why don't you take a look in the mirror?"

Krista sighed and cleared her place. "I don't know what your problem is, but in the future? Why don't you just leave me alone?"

Charlie looked down at her plate. She had been plan-ning on it . . . until a single perfect idea came to her.

"That might be kind of difficult." Charlie shrugged nonchalantly. "Considering we're going to be teammates."

"What are you talking about?" Krista scoffed.

"Oh! You didn't hear?" Charlie asked, feigning igno-rance. "I guess they just fired Coach Harrington and are recruiting some *real* athletes."

"I think I'd know if my own soccer coach got fired," Krista snapped, annoyed.

"It's true." Charlie smirked.

"And you know this how?"

Charlie relished the moment. "Because I was recruited."

She let the shock register on Krista's face before she continued. "But I can't decide what position to go for. Sweeper or maybe striker—"

"*I* play striker," Krista interrupted.

Charlie smiled. "I guess we'll see, won't we?"

Krista's lips pressed together in a thin line. Her face began to turn red.

Charlie just turned her attention back to her dinner. Suddenly, her peas seemed more appetizing. She hadn't really wanted to play soccer, but what the heck? Martie had scouted her, and who was Charlie Brown to argue with destiny?

two

"Unbelievable!" Krista shouted as she hung up the cordless. She'd been listening in on Charlie's phone conversation with Martie, the new soccer coach. What she'd heard was beyond comprehension.

"I told you that you shouldn't eavesdrop," Brooks warned. She snuggled deeper in Krista's papasan chair, the new issue of *Us Weekly* propped up in her lap.

Dressed to go out, Brooks was her usual casual chic in size zero Paper Denim and Cloth jeans and a fitted white James Perse tank top. If anyone could make a wife beater look hot, it was Brooks; of course, the pink lacy bra you could see through the cotton fabric didn't hurt.

Krista grabbed a throw pillow from her bed and wrung it in her hands. Why? Why in the world would Charlie try out for *her* team?

Krista had been on varsity since she was a freshman. Not only did Charlie not *play* soccer anymore, she didn't even *like* soccer. So—why did she have to ruin senior year by dragging her dark cloud over Krista's parade?

Krista frowned. She knew the answer. For the last year,

her sister had made it her mission in life to torture her. And what better way to stress her out than to invade the one place that was totally hers—the soccer field?

Krista clenched her jaw. Things hadn't always been like this. Just a year ago, she and Charlie had been close. Charlie even looked up to her. But last year, all that changed.

Charlie started dressing differently, wearing skate punk clothes instead of the girlie fashions Krista favored. She even talked differently, her words dripping with sarcasm and bile—that was, when she talked at all.

Yep. Charlie was now bitter and spiteful—as though the world had done her wrong—and Krista had no idea why.

Frustrated, she hurled her pillow across the room, narrowly missing Brooks's head.

"Hey!" Brooks exclaimed, using her magazine to shield herself. "Watch where you throw that thing! I have an audition with McG tomorrow."

"Sorry," Krista muttered as she collapsed on her bed. "It's just that it's *my* team. Now there's this new coach and—"

"No way." Brooks sat up, suddenly interested.

"It's true," Krista insisted. "This woman Martie. She—"

"Paris and Stavros? Back together again?" Brooks interrupted. She shook her head at *Us Weekly*. "Double OC."

Brooks loved acronyms and used them obsessively. In Brooks's language, *OC* stood for "out of control." Whatever was out of control about Paris Hilton and Stavros Niarchos was beyond Krista.

"Who cares about them?" Krista snapped. "Didn't you hear me? There's a new soccer coach, and she said that *everyone* has to try out again—even if you've been on the team before—"

"Poor Mary Kate." Brooks sighed. "I think she really loved him, way back when . . ."

Krista sighed. "Missy, are you even listening?"

"Missy" was their special nickname for each other. They'd picked it up from one of Brooks's cousins who lived on the Upper East Side of Manhattan.

Like Brooks's acronyms, "Missy" was a part of their secret code—a language that only the worthy could use. And no one was ever as worthy as Krista and Brooks.

"I've been on this team for three years," Krista continued, "and now I have to earn my spot back? How unfair is that?"

Krista knew the B-dub team wasn't going to win any championships this year. All the other good players had graduated in June. But with even the smallest effort, Krista would end up the star of the squad. Probably the captain. And if she played as well as she had over the summer, she'd probably end up being scouted. How amazing would that look on her college applications?

And now what? Krista wondered. *Now I'm supposed to impress this new person?*

pretty
TOUGH

She bit her lip, worried. What if she *couldn't* impress Martie? What if the new coach figured it out . . . ?

Last year, at the beginning of the season, Krista had torn a ligament. As she raced to get under the ball for a header, she felt a snap in her leg and fell to the ground. The pain was *excruciating*. She'd spent weeks shuttling to the hospital for intense physical therapy.

Krista made it back into full uniform before the end of the season. But since then, she noticed that she played . . . differently. She was more cautious—a little afraid.

No one realized, of course, because Krista's talent made her fear easy to hide. But what if she couldn't hide it from Martie?

"Brooks," she said, horrified. "What if I don't make the team?"

"Who cares?" Brooks smiled as she lazily flipped to another page. "If you don't make it, you'll have more time to hang out with me."

Krista shook her head. She should have known better. When it came to college, Brooks was entirely uninterested . . . unless, of course, it was a college in a movie script. Brooks looked so mature that she'd already played a co-ed, even if the film had gone straight to video.

But Krista wasn't so lucky. Without hard work, her future wasn't straight to anything. She dreamed of following in her dad's footsteps and going to Yale. She thought she had the grades for it, but her dad had been quick to point out that her SAT scores were "nothing to get excited about."

Because of that, everything else *had* to be perfect.

Of course, Krista's determination to go Ivy wasn't only about her dad. It was about Cam too.

Krista and Cam had been girlfriend and boyfriend, officially, for a year and three weeks. Even she had to admit, they made an amazing couple.

Whenever she admired the picture that sat on her dresser—the one they had taken together at Christmas-time—she couldn't help but think that they looked just right. Cam was a few inches taller and as the starting quarterback for B-dub football had a strong, muscular physique. They had similar high cheekbones and a complementary sense of style, and even their blue eyes went well together.

To the other students at Beachwood, they were a golden couple—just meant to be.

Midway through his junior year, Cam had applied early and been accepted at Yale. If Krista had any hope of staying with him, she was going to have to get into Yale too.

Now, as if having her future in the hands of some far-away admissions officer wasn't bad enough, a new coach was going to decide her fate.

"You don't understand," Krista moaned. "This is a disaster."

"You worry too much," Brooks commented, then noticed something in the magazine. "Ooh, look—stripes are the new pink!"

At that moment, Krista couldn't have cared less. "Do you know what the coach told Charlie? We're going to have to run a mile in under seven minutes or we won't make the cut. Seven minutes! I've never run faster than seven thirty-one."

Brooks slammed down her magazine. "Missy, has anyone ever told you to relax?"

Krista hugged a pillow to her chest. Sure, she *had* achieved a certain level of self-awareness, thanks to hours of Bikram yoga, but *mellow* was not a word in her type-A vocabulary.

"Relaxing is not what I do best."

"Missy, you're going to make it," Brooks said, exasperated. "Come on, when have you *not* gotten what you want?"

"What're you talking about?" Krista asked, her voice muffled by the pillow. "*You* get what you want. I get—"

"My sloppy seconds?" Brooks joked.

Krista would have collapsed farther into the pillow had it been possible, knowing of course that Brooks was referring to Cam.

Sophomore year, Cam dated Brooks for three months before she dumped him, setting her sights on someone older. Krista had been the one Cam turned to for comfort.

Cam told Krista repeatedly that getting dumped by Brooks was the best thing that had ever happened to him, but at times it still bothered her. She'd never liked leftovers from the fridge; she certainly didn't like them in a boyfriend.

"I just don't see why we need all these changes," Krista moaned.

"Uh, because the team sucks beyond any reasonable amount of suckage?" Brooks offered.

Sometimes Krista wondered if Brooks enjoyed cutting her down. Well, tonight, she was tired of it.

"You know what else I heard on the phone?" she asked, faux innocently. "They hired a new *assistant* coach too."

Brooks closed *Us Weekly* and looked around, bored. "Do you have *In Touch*? I think Britney's on the cover. What's with the yo-yo dieting?"

Krista reached for the magazine on her desk and tossed it to Brooks. "Not only did they hire a new assistant," she continued, "they hired *Noah Riley*."

Brooks snapped to attention. "Wait—what did you say?"

Krista flipped through Brooks's discarded *Us Weekly* slowly, nonchalantly, as if totally unaware of the way she'd rocked Brooks's world. "Noah Riley's the new volunteer coach," she repeated.

"Noah Riley," Brooks stated. "As in *the* Noah Riley?"

"Unless there's another Noah Riley that didn't give

you the time of day in high school," Krista answered half playfully.

Noah was the senior that Brooks had dumped Cam to date. Even Brooks had to admit, things hadn't panned out the way she'd planned.

Brooks glared at her friend. "Shut up!" She hurled a pillow back in Krista's direction. Krista jumped out of the way as it whapped into the wall.

"Hey!" She laughed. "You're retaliating now?"

"No freaking way!" Brooks yelled. "Noah Riley's back?"

Noah was a bit of a legend around Beachwood, always doing the unexpected. Instead of going off to college like most nineteen-year-olds, he'd gone to Europe to play soccer. He came back a year later, when he suffered a knee injury. Rumor was he'd pretty much healed, but he'd never be the soccer star that he once was.

BANG, BANG, BANG. A thumping came from the other side of the wall.

"Would you guys *shut up?*" Charlie yelled from her bedroom. "I'm trying to sleep in here."

Brooks rolled her eyes.

"Sleep?" Krista shouted back. "It's eight thirty!"

They paused a moment, waiting to see if Charlie would respond.

When she didn't, Brooks shook her head. "What a loser."

"I just—I don't get her." Krista sighed.

Brooks popped up from her chair. "So, are we going to hang out here with your chemically imbalanced sister, or are we going to the party?"

"Definitely party," Krista said. She placed an index finger on her bottom lip. "I wonder if Noah will be there . . . ?"

Brooks raised her eyebrows, then looked Krista up and down. "You're not wearing that, are you?"

Krista scanned her outfit—lime green cords and a white sheer button-down. She loved this outfit. It was straight out of last week's *Seventeen*, with Kirsten Dunst on the cover.

"Oh, this?" she covered. "No way, Missy."

Krista headed into her walk-in closet to search for something better.

Later, when Krista and Brooks were positive the rest of the house was asleep, they began their familiar trek—out Krista's bedroom window, across the roof, down the trellis, and onto the driveway. It had taken a few months of dating Cam for Krista to perfect the art of sneaking out, but now that she had it down pat, Krista didn't stress about it. She did feel a *little* guilty, but her parents were beyond strict when it came to curfews and boyfriends.

Over the summer, she was only allowed to see Cam three times a week and she had to be home by eleven thirty, which was practically daytime for a self-respecting about-to-be senior. If she wanted to continue having a boyfriend and a social life, sneaking out was the only option.

Tonight was the annual End of Summer bonfire, and since Cam was throwing it, it was Krista's duty as his girlfriend to be there. The End of Summer bonfire was legendary at Beachwood. It was always thrown by the captain of the football team, and it usually involved a ridiculously nice beachfront house where the parents were conspicuously absent. Freshmen weren't generally allowed unless they knew somebody, and what happened at the bonfire could make or break you for the following school year.

Three years ago, Amy Wilkinson, a classmate of Krista's, had been the rightful heir to the popularity throne—that was, until she made out with Hannah Jenkins's boyfriend and got blacklisted before school even began. Last year, this total dork, Harvey Harvey (yes, that was his real name) catapulted himself to high school superstardom when he jumped off the roof into the pool . . . and survived.

It was at this party that Krista and Brooks had first met, freshman year (Krista held back Brooks's hair while she was puking up four rum and Diet Cokes). They'd been inseparable ever since.

Cam's parents, the Christiansons, lived in a sprawling house right on the water with their own private beach as their backyard. When the girls pulled into the long, winding driveway, the party was already in full swing. A huge bonfire lit up the beach, and at least two hundred kids were gathered around it. A few guys played beach volleyball, the moon lighting up the net. System of a Down blared from the precariously placed speakers around the deck. Through the large glass windows, Krista could see a group of juniors raiding Cam's parents' bar. Most of the guys didn't bother to use the red plastic cups that Krista and Cam had picked up from Costco the day before, opting instead to drink straight out of the Christiansons' Captain Morgan and Beefeater bottles.

Krista spied Cam near the bar. She waved and started to head inside, but Brooks grabbed her arm.

"Missy," she instructed. "Make him come to you, remember? ABC."

Krista frowned. ABC. Translation: always be cool.

This year, Krista planned to play it cool with Cam. He'd called her "a little clingy" toward the end of junior year, and she'd spent the summer perfecting the art of seeming slightly aloof. She bit her lip nervously—a trait she shared with Charlie—and waited to see if he would actually approach her. In the meantime, a dozen sophomore girls descended upon Brooks.

"Oh my God, you're *Brooks Sheridan!*" one of them squealed. "I loved you in *Girl for Sale.* That's like my favorite movie ever!"

Brooks forced a smile. She'd made that movie for

Disney years ago. It was about a girl who put herself up for adoption on eBay in order to get a new family. Krista knew it was hardly one of Brooks's favorite credits.

Another girl, Regan Holder, turned to Krista. "That skirt is killer."

Krista looked down at her cute Bebe skirt and Anthropologie top. Yes, she'd changed eight times under Brooks's watchful eye. But no one needed to know that.

"Thanks." Krista smiled at Regan's compliment. "It's just something I threw together. . . ."

Krista had known Regan forever—long before Regan ditched Charlie to scale the popularity ladder. Krista couldn't blame her. She would ditch Charlie too if they weren't related.

"Ow!" Krista exclaimed. She felt a stinging sensation on her back. "Who snapped my bra?" she asked, annoyed.

She spun around and found Cam grinning mischievously, showing off his deep dimples. He held a red plastic cup in his hand.

"Beverage?" he offered.

"No thanks," she said, smiling. He wrapped his arms around her waist and nuzzled her neck. He smelled like Speed Stick deodorant, Polo, and pepperoni pizza.

"I missed you," he whispered playfully into her ear. "I'm glad you finally made it."

Krista smiled. "What have you been drinking?" Unlike Cam and his friends, she rarely even took a sip of alcohol.

"Just beer," he replied. "I want to stay sober. I might have to do another run soon."

Harvey walked up, overhearing Cam. "Don't worry, bro. Noah's sober. He offered to go."

Brooks perked up. "Noah's here?" she asked Harvey innocently.

Cam turned his attention back to Krista. "So what took you so long? I thought you'd never get here. . . ."

"My parents were watching *Leno*," she explained. "Didn't you get my text?"

"They probably just used the TV to drown out the sex," Harvey joked.

Krista turned to him. "That is completely disgusting." As far as she was concerned, Harvey could jump off every roof into every pool in Malibu—it still wouldn't make him cool or even tolerable.

"Whatever." Cam shrugged, pulling Krista close. "I'm just glad you're here now." He kissed her, and she melted in his arms. "You look beautiful tonight," he murmured.

Harvey rolled his eyes at the tender moment. "Get a room, dudes."

Cam and Krista pulled apart. Cam smiled, light from the bonfire dancing behind him. "Want to?"

Krista nodded. As they turned to make their way up to the house, she saw Brooks stalk off in search of her prey— Noah Riley.

•   •   •

Two minutes later, Brooks burst into Cam's bedroom. "Missy!" she called, throwing open the door without knocking.

"What're you doing?" Krista exclaimed, breaking away from Cam.

"OMG," Brooks said hurriedly. "I need the number for the new soccer coach—Martie, right?"

Krista looked at her friend as if she was insane. "Now? Why?"

"Because," Brooks stated matter-of-factly, "Operation Noah is in full effect."

Both Krista and Cam stared blankly at Brooks. "Huh?" Krista asked.

Brooks took a deep breath and dramatically paused to emphasize the gravity of what she was about to say.

"Missy, meet your new teammate. I'm trying out for varsity soccer!"

three

When Charlie's alarm clock went off the next morning, she slammed the palm of her hand down onto the snooze button. The last thing she wanted to do was get up and go to school. It was still a week before the start of classes, but because of some last-minute schedule changes (apparently, her parents had an issue with her taking three periods of art in a row), she had to meet with her creepy, close-talking guidance counselor, Mr. Mazula, and change her schedule in person.

Why, why had she stayed out so late last night? It felt almost impossible to lift her head off her pillow.

Last night, she'd heard Brooks and Krista do what they always did—climb out Krista's bedroom window, across the roof, and down the trellis. The lengths to which Krista went to sneak out disgusted Charlie, which was why she did things more simply: she just walked out the front door. No one ever stopped her because no one ever noticed she was leaving.

At eleven forty-five, when she heard Krista's window shut, Charlie quietly crept out of bed, slipped on a sweatshirt, and slid into her flip-flops. Within a minute, she was out on Morningside Lane, heading down to her favorite lifeguard station on the beach.

There were hundreds of stations like it, from Malibu to San Diego, but this one was her favorite. The boy who worked there in the summers was the only lifeguard who didn't have blond hair and blue eyes and a perfectly sculpted body. He looked decidedly unnoticeable—and for that reason alone, Charlie couldn't help but notice him.

They'd never actually spoken, but one time, when she had been pummeled by a particularly big wave, she had seen him running down to the beach toward her. Once he realized she was alive and well, he turned back to his station, but at the time, Charlie wondered what might have happened if she hadn't been so quick to pop out of the water. A lifeguard rescue might have been embarrassing, but think of the perks. Mouth-to-mouth resuscitation? Bring it on!

Granted, it would have been a lame way to get a first kiss, but lips were lips, right?

So last night, she wandered down to the beach, staking out her familiar spot, sitting on the railing of the empty lifeguard station, trying to decide if the blips of light in the sky were stars or planes. It was rare to see stars in LA. At least, the celestial kind. Spotting Britney Spears at Jamba Juice? No biggie. But catching the Big Dipper from a Malibu beach? A practical impossibility! So she contented herself with watching the planes sail toward Los Angeles International Airport.

In the distance, she had heard screams and cheers and blaring music from Cam's party about a quarter of a mile down the beach. Charlie knew that Krista and Brooks were right there—in the middle of it all. She also knew from the moment they started talking about Cam's party—what to wear, who would be there—that she wouldn't be invited. She imagined Regan Holder and her new friends there. The thought made her stomach turn.

Around five in the morning, the sounds of the party finally died down and Charlie made her way back up the road to her house, sneaking back in just as the morning paper hit her driveway. She wondered if Krista was sound asleep in her bed and considered checking to see if she was home.

Ultimately, she decided against it: she wasn't responsible for Krista, and since last year it was more than obvious that Krista felt no responsibility toward her. For all intents and purposes, each of them was an only child.

BANG, BANG, BANG. A knock at her bedroom door interrupted her sleepy thoughts, bringing her back to the cold, hard reality of her early morning obligation.

"Charlie," her mom cooed. "You're going to be late for your meeting."

"I know," Charlie muttered as she pulled the covers

farther over her head. "I just need ten more minutes. Just ten more—"

BANG, BANG, BANG! Her mom knocked again, even more firmly. "I mean it," she snapped. "Get up. Now."

"I'm coming!" Charlie yelled, exasperated. Why did her mom even care if she wanted to take art classes all day long? Weren't parents supposed to want their children to be happy? Of course, if her parents *had* really wanted her to be happy, they would have given her a name like Kaitlin or Lindsey.

Interestingly, Charlie's parents had taken more notice of her since she mentioned she'd been recruited for the soccer team. Her father was a soccer fanatic, and he and Krista had grown close over the years, practicing timing and passing drills in their backyard. What seemed to have become a way for Krista and her dad to bond made Charlie feel decidedly left out. Well, no more. Not after Charlie not only made the team, but beat the Juicy Couture pants right off Krista.

Throwing back the covers, Charlie looked at her reflection in the mirror mounted on her wall: brown hair sticking up in every direction, red puffy eyes . . . even her freckles seemed to be messier than usual.

Out in the hallway, Krista pranced by, her hair, skin, and clothes all perfect.

"Mom," she called out. "Brooks is here. We're going to the mall."

Charlie couldn't believe it. It was so unfair. Krista could do whatever she wanted today while Charlie had to visit that yawning pit of despair known as Beachwood High. She glanced back at her own reflection and told herself that it was okay. Crappy days like this were going to make the day she stole Krista's place on the soccer team that much sweeter. Not that she had any intention of ever joining the team . . . but Krista didn't need to know that. It would make torturing her a lot less fun.

Walking through the halls of Beachwood, Charlie felt like she had never left. School wasn't in session, but she could still smell the lingering stench of fiesta salad and Salisbury steak—staples of the Beachwood cafeteria—wafting through the corridor. Her stomach gave a tiny warning heave. Juniors and seniors were allowed to go off campus for lunch and could hit the Starbucks or Carl's Jr. nearby, but as a sophomore Charlie was still relegated to the lunch line and the perils of the high school cafeteria.

Forget the dangers of South Central or Compton. Try navigating around Regan and her clique of football players and cheerleaders. If your IQ didn't drop twenty points just by being within a two-foot radius of them, your self-esteem surely did.

Charlie shuddered at the thought as she rounded the corner and pushed open the glass doors to the guidance office. There, her fate (or at least her schedule for the next nine months of her life) would be decided.

Inside, the guidance office smelled like a potent mix of college applications, schedule changes, and desperation. Even with the air-conditioning lightly blowing through the vents, the August heat was stifling. Charlie wondered if it was already too hot for the beach. She should have gotten up earlier this morning, when the waves were at their best.

Charlie told the receptionist in the guidance office that she was there and reluctantly took a seat next to an overweight boy, likely a freshman, who seemed to be working up a sweat just sitting in the orange plastic chair.

After a thirty-minute wait, her name was finally called.

"Charlie Brown?" The receptionist sneered, more than a hint of sarcasm in her voice. Charlie glared at her, wishing her a lifetime of career mediocrity and carpal tunnel syndrome, then slunk into Mr. Mazula's office.

The ten minutes she spent with Mr. Mazula, who reeked of an odd combination of cigarettes and pickles, seemed endless but resulted in a new and improved schedule (if you considered the removal of two art classes "improved").

As Charlie hurriedly left his office, she looked over her classes. She had Miss Reese for English. Strange, because according to Krista, Mrs. Cryer taught all sophomore English classes. She also noticed that she had Mr. Castillo for "Choices and Challenges," which she'd heard was just a fancy way to say sex ed. She remembered Krista taking driver's ed from Mr. Castillo and wondered why the same person typically taught both, as if the two went hand in hand.

Whatever. Charlie had no time to ponder. All she knew was that she couldn't wait to get out of there.

She pushed through the front doors. Finally . . . freedom!

She picked up her pace and—*oof!*—ran smack into someone.

"Charlie, whoa," Martie exclaimed, the stack of books in her hands tumbling to the floor. "Where's the fire?"

"Sorry," Charlie apologized, kneeling down to help gather the books. She noticed that they all had the same title: *To Kill a Mockingbird.*

"You must really like this one," she joked.

Martie smiled. "Let's hope my students do." She grabbed the last remaining book and stood up.

Charlie stared at Martie. Her *students?* "Wait. Soccer doesn't have some sort of twisted reading requirement, does it?"

Martie laughed. "Of course not. You mind helping me carry these down to my classroom?"

"Classroom?" Charlie asked. "Hold on . . ." She fumbled for her schedule. "You're—"

"—taking over Mrs. Cryer's English classes," Martie filled in as she strolled down the hallway.

Charlie caught up to her. "*You're* Miss Reese? I have you for English!"

Martie explained that Mrs. Cryer decided not to come back after her maternity leave, and Charlie stifled a smile. Krista was going to be so jealous when Charlie told her she had an inside line to the new soccer coach . . . that, in fact, she'd be seeing her in class Monday through Friday. Imagine the bonding potential—teacher *and* coach! Not to mention that she'd escaped the wrath of Mrs. Cryer, who had given Krista her first and only C. It was too good to be true!

Charlie followed Martie into the classroom and set the stack of books down on a desk. She glanced around. The classroom was completely bare.

"I wanted to hang some posters and inspiring quotes around the room," Martie explained. "I've just been so busy with everything, I've barely had time to get the place ready. All I have is that dumb kitten poster. You know, the one where the kitten is hanging from a tree branch and it says—"

"Hang in there?" Charlie guessed.

"That's the one. And if I put that up, I'll be crucified. 'Hang in there' posters are strictly the domain of—"

"Mrs. Kennedy," Charlie said, finishing Martie's thought. "Krista says it's been in her classroom for three years straight. She's never taken it down."

Martie laughed. "Got that right. She hung that poster up when *I* went here."

Charlie laughed too . . . then waited awkwardly. "Well, um . . . if there's nothing else you need . . ." She edged toward the door.

"Actually, there is *one* thing I could use your help with," Martie added. "If you have time."

Charlie looked at her watch, considering. She wished she had somewhere to be—a friend's house, a date, anything to remotely indicate she was a normal teenage girl—but the truth was, with no friends and no place to go, Charlie had nothing *but* time.

Forty-five minutes later, Martie and Charlie pulled up to a run-down field in South Central, Los Angeles. Charlie bit her lip as she looked around. Although she'd heard of South Central and had even studied the race riots that had happened there back in the early nineties, she'd never actually seen it. Or been near it. In fact, she rarely left Malibu.

Brooks always joked that heading a few miles south to Pacific Palisades, Santa Monica, or Venice was "slummin' it." Charlie wondered what Brooks would say about this place.

Martie turned off the ignition and unfastened her seat belt. Charlie sat still in the passenger seat, unsure of what to do. She stared at the field where a soccer game was in progress—four guys against two guys and a girl. Charlie could hear the players yelling in Spanish, instructing each other and cheering as the lone girl dribbled the ball around a defender. She faked left, dashed right, and shot the ball between the two tires set up as a makeshift goal.

"Wooooo!" the girl cheered, and pumped her fist.

"Did you see that?" Martie asked excitedly. She climbed out of the car, then noticed Charlie's hesitation.

"It's fine if you want to wait here," Martie offered, leaning in the window, "but there's nothing to be scared of."

Charlie recoiled at the veiled accusation. She wasn't *scared*. Even if she was the only white person in sight. She wasn't like Brooks and the other trust fund brats at Beachwood, who cared only about people's appearances.

Charlie got out of the car and followed Martie toward the chain-link fence surrounding the field. Martie looked so comfortable, so self-assured as she strode toward the gate. Charlie realized her own shoulders were up around her ears. She willed herself to relax. *Take longer strides,* she told herself. *Breathe.*

"Carla!" Martie shouted, just as the game was about to resume. The girl looked over and gave a wave. She said something to the boys in Spanish and sprinted over to the fence.

Charlie heard sirens blaring in the distance. She shoved her hands deeper into her pockets.

"You came back!" Carla smiled happily from the other side of the fence, then pointed to Charlie. "With a friend."

Charlie stared at Carla enviously. With her olive-colored

skin and big brown eyes, Carla practically glowed. Even though it was pulled back in a loose ponytail, her thick brown hair looked straight out of a shampoo commercial—long and shiny. For all the darkness and bitterness that Charlie could feel spilling out of her pores, Carla had a completely opposite disposition—sweetness and light radiated from her broad smile.

Martie introduced them. "Carla Hernandez, Charlie Brown."

Carla giggled as she reached back and grabbed the top of her foot for a quad stretch. "That's a joke, ri—"

"My parents have an evil sense of humor," Charlie stated. She wondered for the hundredth time if she had grounds to sue for emancipation. A name like hers *had* to be a form of child abuse.

"Have you had a chance to talk to your mother yet?" Martie asked Carla, interrupting Charlie's internal rant.

"Yes, and we both really appreciate your coming all the way out here," Carla explained. She tilted her head and blocked the sun from her eyes. "But she's just not sure . . ."

Martie jumped in quickly. "Is your mom home? Because I have the scholarship information in the car, and I think once she sees it laid out and understands where kids who go to Beachwood end up—"

"It's not just my mom," Carla interrupted. "It's me too." She shrugged, suddenly uncomfortable. "I don't know. I'm just not sure I'd really fit in." She glanced at Charlie. "No offense."

Charlie shrugged. "None taken."

"You obviously wanted a change when you submitted an application last spring," Martie prodded.

"I know," Carla mumbled. "It's just . . . Malibu? Look at me. I don't belong in Malibu."

"Hey," Martie said sternly. "You belong wherever you want to belong. Where do you think I went to high school?"

Carla looked at Martie, surprised. "Beachwood?"

Martie nodded. "All four years. Commuted from Crenshaw. It wasn't always easy, but it was the right decision. I would never have had the same opportunities in my neighborhood . . . which doesn't make it right. It's just the truth, you know?"

One of the boys called from the field. "Carla, you playing? Sí o no?"

"Sí, sí," Carla responded. "Uno momento."

"You go," Martie said. "Let me discuss this with your mom. And then you and I can talk some more."

Carla agreed. "Okay, thanks."

Martie turned to cross the street, then looked back over her shoulder. "Charlie—why don't you join in? Looks like their side could use an extra player."

Charlie glanced at the guys nervously.

Carla beamed. "You play too?"

"Uh . . ." Charlie wavered. "I used to. Haven't played in a while."

Carla ran back toward the field. "Well, I guess a while's up. Come on."

Charlie watched her go and made a quick decision. She climbed up and hopped over the chain-link fence, joining in a game for the first time in years.

"Here ya go," Carla said triumphantly, handing Charlie a cherry-flavored snow cone. "Girls rule, boys drool."

Charlie laughed. She and Carla had won their game six to two. Carla's two older brothers, their teammates, had been particularly impressed when Charlie assisted Carla in three consecutive goals. It was the most fun she'd had all summer long.

"How much do I owe you?" Charlie asked, taking the snow cone. With the afternoon sun beating down and the temperature creeping into the upper nineties, the cone looked especially delicious. She took a huge, icy bite. It was so cold it made the inside of her mouth numb.

"I got it," Carla responded. "My brother's girlfriend works at the stand."

Charlie looked over at the girl behind the stand. She was so pregnant she looked like she was about to burst.

"Thank you," Charlie replied through another mouthful of ice. She nodded toward the field. "You were awesome out there. I can see why Martie wants you for the team."

"So you're definitely playing?" Carla asked. "For Beachwood?"

Charlie shrugged. "Martie recruited me to try out, but I haven't really played soccer in over a year."

"Growing up, I just played with my brothers in the street or here," Carla confessed. "I've never actually been on a team before."

"Not even at school?" Charlie asked. It seemed impossible that a girl this good had never played on a real team.

Carla laughed. "At my school, we're lucky if we all get desks."

"Well, if you go to Beachwood, you can have my desk . . . in all of my classes," Charlie grumbled. "I hate that place. I wouldn't say this in front of Martie, but you're smart not to go there."

"You think?" Carla wondered, peering over her shoulder at her apartment complex.

"To the people at Beachwood, there's all this *stuff* that matters," Charlie said. "You know, who your parents are, what kind of car you drive. . . . It's all so superficial. I mean, who cares?"

"I guess," Carla agreed. "I don't know. It sounds superficial, but when you don't have it? All those opportunities . . . Maybe I care." She shrugged, her expression unsure. "Anyway, Malibu—it's so far away."

Charlie nodded in agreement. "It took us an hour to

get out here, and it wasn't even rush hour. Imagine how long the bus would take."

"That's the crazy thing," Carla explained. "Martie said they'd provide the transportation."

Charlie was impressed. She wondered if Martie could get *her* a ride too. That way, she wouldn't have to ride with her sister.

"So what's it really like there?" Carla asked. "I mean, the other kids."

"Oh, they're the worst!" Charlie answered, her opinions pouring out of her like water. "The jocks strut around thinking they're God's gift to the universe, and the biggest stress in their lives is whether to wear boxers or briefs. And the girls are even worse. It's all about how you dress and who you know and who you're hooking up with. Most of them don't have an original thought in their head—much less their own body parts. Four girls in my class got nose jobs just last semester. And there are so many fake boobs, we should just call ourselves Silicone Valley."

"Wow," Carla said. "Guess you're kind of unhappy there."

"Unhappy doesn't even come close," Charlie stated matter-of-factly. "There isn't a word in the English language to describe what I think of that place."

"Well, it can't be all bad," Carla offered. "I mean, you don't seem like any of those kids you described."

Charlie shrugged. "I keep my distance."

"What about your friends?" Carla asked. "Do they keep their distance too?"

"My friends . . ." Charlie struggled to find the words, then just blurted it out. "I don't have any friends there."

Carla smiled and tipped the last bit of snow cone into her mouth. "Well, who knows . . . maybe you do now."

Charlie finished her snow cone quickly, keeping the red cherry syrup from dripping on her shorts. As she savored the last cool shavings, she smiled. She didn't want to jinx it, but maybe, just maybe, her days of eating fish sticks alone in the cafeteria were over.

Charlie made a mental note: Even if Carla didn't transfer, she should stop eating the fish sticks anyway.

four

"Come on!" Krista commanded as she grabbed her car keys off the kitchen counter.

Charlie ate her Cookie Crisp, taking one slow, determined bite at a time. "You have somewhere to be or something?" she chided, her mouth full of milk and cereal.

Krista tapped her foot, annoyed, her backpack and soccer bag already slung over her shoulder. The way Charlie acted, you'd think she was four years younger than Krista instead of the twenty-two months that actually stood between them.

"Charlie, stop fooling around. I'm serious. We have to go."

Charlie spooned another bite into her mouth. "In a minute," she said. She looked up at Krista. "You're not actually wearing *that*, are you?"

Krista looked down at her carefully chosen outfit—boho sheer top over a white tank with worn-in True Religion jeans and beaded Planet Blue sandals. A thick chunky beaded necklace and gigantic Mary-Kate sunglasses capped off the look.

"What's wrong with it?" Krista asked defensively. She'd been up since five o'clock in the morning, rooting through her closet, determined to pick out the perfect first-day-of-senior-year outfit. She had to look good. All eyes would be on her. She'd already IM'ed Brooks with several possibilities and now, right when she was actually feeling confident, Charlie was trying to undermine her.

Rude!

Charlie didn't answer, but Krista had had enough. "Fine, whatever. I'm leaving. I'm not going to be late on my first day because of you."

She strode out the back door and headed to the car. She threw her bags in the trunk and slammed it shut. She opened the driver's side door and glanced over at the kitchen window where Charlie still sat, eating her stupid Cookie Crisp, totally unfazed. Krista shook her head. You couldn't pay her to consume that much sugar in one sitting.

She jammed her key into the ignition, starting her Jetta. She looked again. Charlie hadn't budged. She debated giving one last honk, then reconsidered. She wasn't her sister's keeper. In fact, she didn't even feel like her sister's *sister*. It was as if she lived with a virtual stranger.

Fine, Charlie could just be that way. Krista shut her door and peeled out of the driveway, making a sharp right turn onto the street. She wasn't going to let her sister ruin her first day of senior year . . . or any day after that.

Pulling into the senior parking lot, into a prime space right by the math wing, Krista felt elated. She'd just hung up with Brooks, who was still a few minutes away. They always spent their ride to school talking on the phone. It made Krista wonder what people did in cars before cell phones—driving was so boring!

As she popped the trunk and got out of her car, she saw Cam across the lot, surrounded by a group of giddy sophomore girls. Krista felt a familiar pang of jealousy as she watched Regan Holder squeal in delight and give him a hug.

It couldn't be helped, really. When your boyfriend is the captain of the football team, every girl wants to get with him.

Krista shook her head. It was just a few days ago that Regan had drunkenly spilled vodka and cranberry juice all over Brooks's dry-clean-only BCBG top at Cam's party. What a loser. Maybe she and Charlie *should* have been best friends.

"Hey, Cam," Krista called out, giving him a casual, I'm-totally-cool-with-Regan-mauling-you wave. She was about to head over to him when she remembered Brooks's instructions: *ABC, Missy. Always be cool. Make him come to you.*

She waited, wondering if he would. Then she saw Regan grab his hand.

Okay. Playing it cool only went so far. She took a deep breath and glanced at her watch. It was only ten minutes until the bell, and she needed to mark her territory. As she marched toward the sophomore gigglers, she suppressed a smile, thinking that if she were a golden retriever, she'd simply pee on Cam, ending all debate about the matter. As it was, she'd have to do things the hard way.

Nudging herself between Cam and Regan, she wrapped her arms around Cam's neck.

"Hey, baby," she murmured, looking deep into his eyes.

"Hey, hotness," Cam responded.

Now she had his attention.

"Hi, Krista," Regan chirped. "Fun party, huh?"

Krista turned and forced a smile. "It was all right. There were a few too many sloppy people by the end. It's sooo embarrassing when people can't control themselves."

Regan glanced down at her shoes.

Krista wasn't going to feel bad about embarrassing her. Ditching Charlie was one thing. Krista could forgive Regan that, even though, truth be told, she had done it in a pretty nasty way. But flirting with Cam? That was quite another.

"You look gorgeous," Cam said. He gave Krista a long, slow kiss.

They broke apart, and Krista flashed a smile at the sophomore girls. Her smile was one of her best features. Her teeth were perfectly straight and white and, unlike Charlie, she'd never had to wear braces. Their family dentist, Dr. Payne, had even told her she had absolutely perfect teeth.

"So, ready?" she asked Cam sweetly. "I want to go to my locker before first period. I told Brooks we'd meet her."

"Sure, let's go." Cam grabbed her soccer bag and slung it over his shoulder. "Senior year awaits."

The sophomores looked disappointed, Regan most of all.

Game, set, and match, Krista thought. As they made their way inside the school, she wondered—why did Regan Holder bother her so much? And what did Krista really have to be jealous about? *She* was the one with the hot boyfriend. *She* was one of the most popular girls in the entire school. Sure, her soccer thighs were getting a little too muscular . . . and she could definitely pinch an inch on the underside of her arms . . . but she could do something about that, and she would as soon as . . .

"Missy!" Brooks yelled to Krista from halfway down the hall. Krista turned and glanced over her shoulder.

"Hi, Missy." She waved, right as the first bell rang. She crammed her soccer bag into her locker and turned to face Cam, who planted another huge kiss on her lips. Krista melted into him. God, he was so hot.

pretty
TOUGH

"You guys," Brooks admonished as she approached. "Rent a room."

"Everyone says that," Krista teased. "Really, Missy, it's so unoriginal."

"So are your sloppy make-out sessions," Brooks countered.

"I've got a room. How 'bout the janitor's closet?" Cam suggested, raising his eyebrows seductively. "After third period."

Krista playfully hit him. "You wish."

"Yeah, I do," he said, grabbing her again and pulling her close.

"Ew!" Brooks pushed him off Krista. "Okay, massive PDA? SNC."

Cam gave Brooks a blank stare. Krista decided to translate. "Public displays of affection," she told him. "So not cool."

Cam raised his eyebrows at Krista. "She's just jealous. I heard Noah didn't give her the time of day at my party."

Brooks's jaw dropped at the accusation. Krista's eyes widened in horror. She should have warned Cam not to go there. Brooks had been on a rampage since that night, hounding Krista to share everything she knew about soccer. They'd even gone shopping for new cleats and shin guards.

"Ex-ca-use me?" Brooks asked, adding a syllable to emphasize how offended she was.

Cam shrugged. "Don't take it out on us just because you're not getting any."

Brooks's eyes narrowed into two little slits. "You know what?" she said between clenched teeth. "I'd be offended if I thought you were getting some. But everyone knows you're dating Miss Virginity here, so—"

"Brooks!" Krista exclaimed, beyond horrified.

"At least she's not a total whore, like *you,*" Cam shot back.

Brooks lunged at him just as the second bell rang.

"Oh my God! You guys." Krista stepped in between them. "Stop." She turned to Brooks. "Listen, he didn't mean that."

"Yes, I did," Cam disagreed. "I meant it. She'd get with any guy she thought would improve her image—"

"Okay, we're late. We should really go," Krista interrupted.

Brooks stormed off toward the English wing.

"Cam—" Krista began. He shook his head and stalked off in the other direction, leaving Krista alone at her locker.

She didn't understand why the two people closest to her still got so riled up at each other. They'd barely even dated. If Krista didn't know better, she'd guess that they still had feelings for each other. . . .

Great, Krista thought. *Now you're* imagining *things to worry about.*

She slammed the locker door shut. Hard. And ran to catch up with a very pissed-off Brooks.

Charlie biked toward Beachwood and finally saw it looming at the top of the hill. The school, beautiful but menacing, was housed in two large Spanish-style buildings. Both had indoor hallways lined with lockers and outdoor walkways surrounding grassy areas with picnic tables and trees. Krista said it looked a lot like a smaller version of Stanford's campus when she visited.

"Get a good look while you're visiting," Charlie had teased, as Krista left for her college tour, "because you're never getting in there."

Outside the school were two separate parking lots— one for teachers and faculty, another for students. There were practice fields for sports, a field house with a weight room and full-length pool, and a stadium where athletes could play night games under the lights. From the upper-most bleacher, you could see that the school was perched at the top of a cliff, overlooking the Pacific Ocean. But to Charlie, it didn't make a difference. No matter how pretty you made the package, school was still school.

She arrived on campus late, halfway through first period. She steered her bike into the empty bike rack and padlocked it to the metal rails, cursing Krista's name under her breath in the process. She wondered how she could be related to such a monster. Maybe she would ask her parents for genetic testing for Christmas in order to prove that she was the victim of some twisted mistake. She couldn't actually share DNA with Krista. And if she did? Well, that was one of the great injustices of the universe.

She unzipped her backpack and pulled out her schedule to see what class she was missing and where she needed to be next. Missing: English. Next: Choices and Challenges. She thought of going to her locker to kill time but realized she had no idea what the combination was. Students were assigned lockers for all four years and were encouraged to write the combination in a "safe, secure location."

At the time, the sole of Charlie's Converse sneaker had seemed as secure a location as any. Too bad they were stolen at the beach this summer.

She looked at her watch and decided to wait for second period. Walking into English late on the first day of school was like sending an invitation for ridicule to the entire class. She'd had enough of that during her freshman year to last a lifetime. She'd rather wait it out.

The bell rang for second period. Kids pushed through the classroom doors, flooding the perimeter of the school. Most students opted to walk outside whenever possible. Some kids went to smoke by the Dumpster behind the cafeteria. The thought grossed Charlie out. Smoking felt so nineties.

pretty
TOUGH

Pushing through the doors of Beachwood and seeing all the familiar faces, Charlie's stomach churned. She kept her head down and barreled through the hallway.

Her mission: Get to class.

Her goal: Survive the year.

Maybe this would be the year when no one scrawled lies about her on the bathroom wall. She had Regan to thank for that. Charlie's entire body tensed up at the thought. She remembered that day in the cafeteria last year like it was yesterday. . . .

December 17, Charlie walked into the caf after getting a text from Regan canceling the sleepover they'd been planning for ages. They were supposed to stay up all night and watch the Molly Ringwald movies from the eighties that they'd never seen. But Nick, Regan's new boyfriend, had invited her to a party, and in what had become par for the course, she'd decided to ditch Charlie. Well, Charlie had finally had enough. She and Regan had been best friends since they were *seven*. Charlie was sick of pretending she didn't care that her best friend was virtually MIA. And ditching your friends as soon as you got a boyfriend? How disgustingly cliché was that?

But as soon as Charlie confronted Regan, she knew it was the biggest mistake of her life.

"*God*. Sorry I can't sleep over," Regan had said, hardly sorry at all. "It's not like there won't be a million other chances."

"That's not the point," Charlie had replied, her voice naturally rising to talk over the chatter in the cafeteria. "We had plans."

"That's the thing about plans. They change." Regan sighed, as if she couldn't bother to be bothered.

"Yeah, plans change," Charlie snapped. "But not constantly. Not all the time, *every time* you make them."

Other kids at her table stopped what they were talking about to listen.

Regan looked her up and down. "What is your problem anyway?"

"My *problem* is that ever since you got a boyfriend, you act like I don't exist." Charlie tried to stay calm but her heart was racing. She didn't like confrontation, especially in front of people. What was she thinking, starting in with Regan here in the cafeteria?

"I *knew* you were jealous," Regan had snapped. "Just because I have a boyfriend and you don't."

"I'm not jealous," Charlie had shot back. "I don't even want a stupid boyfriend. All I want is—"

"What? To have me all to yourself?" Regan interrupted. "God, Charlie. Should I warn Nick he has some competition?"

The girls at her table laughed, as if they were all in on some joke Charlie didn't understand. "What are you talking about?"

Regan's voice soared above everyone else's. "I knew your

name was Charlie, but I didn't think you were *one of the boys*."

Charlie's face burned with humiliation. The girls at her table laughed louder.

"I'm just saying—" Regan herself laughed now. "Well, some girls might appreciate you having a *thing* for them, but I'm not one of them."

The accusation was ridiculous. Charlie didn't have a "thing" for Regan. She just didn't understand why her best friend constantly ditched her. Didn't she have a right to know?

She heard the taunting laughter of the other kids and felt like a million eyes were on her.

Charlie turned and saw Krista a few tables over, gazing at her impassively. Couldn't she see what was going on here? Why wouldn't she do anything?

Her head spinning, Charlie hadn't been able to see or think. Instead, she did the one thing that came naturally: if someone pushed her, she pushed back.

Charlie lunged at Regan. She shoved her hard and watched her topple back over her chair. With a thud, she landed on the ugly linoleum floor.

Charlie glanced over her shoulder at Krista, who shook her head and returned to her conversation as though nothing had happened.

Within five minutes, Charlie had been given a week's suspension. Too bad it hadn't been a lifetime. She knew she would never be able to go back and face everyone who'd jeered and laughed at what Regan said about her.

But eventually, of course, she had to go back. That was when things went from bad to worse. She heard girls snickering behind her in hallways—boys saying rude things to her when she stood in the lunch line or gathered her books at her locker—lies written about her on the bathroom walls.

Charlie shut it all out. She wanted to be invisible and, after keeping her head down and barely making eye contact with anyone for the second half of her freshman year, she'd succeeded.

She planned to continue that strategy as a sophomore, which was why walking into Choices and Challenges was disturbing on so many levels. Hurtful comments made in her direction were practically guaranteed. The poster inside the classroom asking, *Are you depressed?* didn't help.

Keeping her eyes averted, she made her way to a desk in the back row, aiming to blend into the bookshelves behind her. She scanned the books on the shelf. *Sex and the Zitty: A Teen's Guide Through the Ups and Downs of Adolescence.*

Riveting.

As she sat down, she noticed someone staring at her.

Charlie sighed. It had started already. Someone was staring and . . . *smiling?*

Charlie looked up. There, on the other side of the

room—an oasis in a desert, a life raft in the ocean. Carla!

"Hey," Charlie said timidly, giving a little half wave.

Carla's grin broke into a wide smile. She gathered up her stuff and switched to a desk right next to Charlie.

"Hey," she said. "I was hoping we'd have class together."

The janitor's closet was the last place Krista should have been at two fifteen in the afternoon. She knew that. She had been on her way to her first soccer practice when Cam grabbed her and pulled her inside.

It was funny . . . and romantic . . . and horrible because she knew she was really late. After fifteen minutes, she insisted that she really had to go.

"One more kiss," Cam said. "What's the rush?"

"The rush is I'm supposed to be at practice," Krista explained again. "It's not like last year. All these girls have been recruited and—"

"I know." Cam groaned, pulling away. "The team. It's all I've been hearing about for five days. What about me? Shouldn't you worry about me more than soccer?"

Krista sighed. "I'm sorry. I have to go. I'll call you tonight."

"Okay," Cam finally conceded, "but I'm serious. You owe me."

Krista didn't stop to think what that meant. With a final peck on the lips, she slipped away from Cam and out of the closet.

She ran down the hallway and pushed through the doors to the athletics field. The team hopefuls were already gathered there. Martie, the new coach, stood in front of them, mid-speech. Krista's heart began to race. The start of a new season was always exciting.

"I'd like to welcome everyone to our first official practice," Martie said happily. As if on cue, all the girls applauded. "For those of you who don't know, my name is Martie Reese. And I graduated from B-dub in 1994."

Krista couldn't help but be surprised that Martie had gone to Beachwood. The student body had little diversity. From the looks of the team, though, that was starting to change.

The recruits were a virtual melting pot—a tiny Asian girl with her hair pulled into two short, pointy ponytails, an African American girl with the most developed triceps Krista had ever seen, a beautiful Hispanic girl cracking her knuckles, and—Krista narrowed her eyes, her heart sinking as she saw:

Charlie.

So she *was* serious about tryouts. Well, that was really a shame. Krista was going to have to crush that dream immediately. No way was she going to share the field with her sister. She would rather wear size-three cleats and have her fingernails pulled out one by one than have Charlie steal her spotlight out of spite.

She watched as Charlie whispered something to the knuckle-cracking girl next to her.

Krista shook her head in disbelief. What was *this?* Was the Apocalypse upon her? It had to be the end of the world if Charlie, a self-imposed social outcast, was actually speaking to someone.

Krista snapped her attention back to Martie's speech.

"After that, I became a member of the U.S. National team," Martie continued. "In the last few years I've returned to coaching, and I'm really excited to be back at Beachwood. I know many of you were on the team last year, and I'm glad you're here with us today. We're also fortunate to have talented, skilled student athletes from all across Los Angeles—brand-new students at Beachwood—trying out, as well as a few girls from Beachwood's other teams."

Really? Krista thought. She glanced around the crowd again, confused. On one side of the semicircle, Brooks had positioned herself right next to Noah. Not surprising.

On the opposite side, Krista saw her two good friends and teammates, Buffi and Julie . . . but Martie wasn't kidding. Girls from other sports *were* trying out for soccer.

Jen, a senior from the beach volleyball team, and Karen and Heather, two junior standouts from the track team, were seated in the middle of the bench. Karen was Beachwood's top cross-country runner and Heather, a record-holding sprinter.

Did these girls actually think they could just walk in and play a sport that Krista had been playing for her entire life? So what if they played when they were, like, ten? Like

Charlie, they were going to be sorely disappointed when the team was picked.

"You girls are all athletes in every sense of the word," Martie continued. "It's not the sport that makes you successful as an athlete; it's being an athlete that makes you successful in the sport. That warrior mentality, that sense of pride you get from doing something to the best of your ability, cannot be learned. That's something you already have within yourself. My job is to help you bring it out on the soccer field. My job as your coach is to develop high-caliber soccer players and bring recognition back to a program that was once great. But more than that, my job is to develop amazing young women who take pride in themselves and their school."

Krista sighed, a little too loudly. Sure, pride was well and good, but the truth was, Beachwood's record was bound to be mediocre this year. Krista tried not to let it get to her. If anything, it helped her stand out more among her classmates. She knew she was a great player, but at Beachwood she could also be the star.

Did Martie think she could waltz in here and revamp the entire team? In just six weeks?

Good luck, Krista thought. Their old coach had been trying for four years.

As Martie droned on, Krista glanced at her watch, wondering if they were even going to play. If not, she'd have to cancel her plans with Cam later to go for a run instead. Brooks and Krista always made sure to get at least forty minutes of cardio in six days a week. After all, it was bathing suit season all year long in SoCal.

"I want you to know that whether or not you make the team does not determine your value as an athlete or human being. That said, I can only take seventeen of you for varsity, and whether you were on the team last year, were recruited, or are a walk-on, you're going to have to prove yourself and earn your spot. I know many of you have given up playing a fall sport or competing for a club team in order to be dedicated to Beachwood soccer. Those sacrifices do not go unnoticed, but it will take complete dedication, extreme effort, and superior skills to make this team. What you get back will be even greater than what you could imagine. This is going to be the year that, together, we put Beachwood women's soccer on the map!"

Martie's energy created a ripple effect in the group; her enthusiasm was contagious. The girls applauded excitedly. Krista was immune. It was easy to give a speech; it was another thing to actually coach. Martie's instinct in that department was clearly questionable, given the players she recruited . . . or, at least, one player.

"Now, I'm sure many of you have heard of hell week. It's not only a chance to get in top physical shape," Martie explained, "but an opportunity to bond with your future teammates while I'm kicking your butts."

Everyone laughed nervously.

Krista knew all about hell week. It was essentially boot camp—an intense round of pre-season training where the girls' abilities and skills were tested and noted. And although it was called "hell *week*," it was technically only five days.

Krista loved hell week because it gave her a chance to shine. She worked harder than any other girl and had the body and skills to show for it.

"I'm going to post a list after hell week of the girls who've made the team.

"And then," Martie added, "those who are on the list will begin hell *month*."

Krista's jaw dropped.

"What do you mean, hell month?" Brooks snapped, not liking the sound of the phrase.

Beside her, Noah smirked. "Um, hell week times four?"

Brooks smiled playfully, reversing course. "Well, I knew *that*." She smacked him lightly on the shoulder. "Silly."

Krista rolled her eyes. Martie continued.

"Every day after school, we'll meet either here on the practice field or at Zuma or Pepperdine, depending on our conditioning focus. We'll run, scrimmage, do drills. And on Saturday mornings, for those who live locally, I'll set up optional canyon runs for anyone who's interested."

Krista breathed a sigh of relief at the word *optional*. It

looked like weekends were going to be her only time to see Cam.

"And by optional," Martie added, "I mean *be there*."

The girls looked at each other nervously. Krista cast a sideways glance at Charlie. This was going to cut into her sister's surf time, which would normally drive her crazy. Maybe she would drop out right now. . . .

No such luck. Charlie's lips pressed together, forming a firm line. Her stubborn look. She appeared completely determined, committed, and unfazed by Martie's demands. Krista took a deep breath and tried to wipe the look of concern off her face. With all the girls assembled, it looked like she *was* going to have some serious competition after all.

five

Peering out of her bedroom window the next morning, Charlie thought she was still asleep and dreaming. Down below her stood Carla, next to a sleek black Town Car with its very own driver, Martie's Uncle Roger. Although he lived near downtown LA, Roger worked for a company that was based in Malibu, so he made the trip to the water on a daily basis. Using money from the new school soccer endowment, Martie had arranged for him to drive any girls who lived far away to Beachwood, including Carla.

Carla waved at Charlie. Charlie opened her window and stuck out her head.

"What are you doing here?" she called, confused.

"You missed first period yesterday," Carla said, as though her showing up was the most natural thing in the world. "So I thought I'd give you a ride. That way you don't have to rely on . . ." Carla thought for a moment, trying to recall Charlie's own words. "What did you call her?"

Charlie thought about it. The possibilities were endless. A sheep? A lemming? Suddenly, it came to her.

"The Wicked Witch of the West Side?" she offered.

"That was it." Carla laughed. Loud and unapologetic, the sound rang out like a bell. "That way you don't have to rely on your sister."

Charlie felt elated. This was the closest thing she'd had to a friend in what felt like forever. She couldn't go through another year without anyone to talk to, having people call her a mute, and saying she should ride the short bus.

How awesome, she thought, *to show up in a chauffeured car instead.*

"Give me five minutes," she yelled. She slammed her window shut and threw on an old pair of cords and her vintage Black Sabbath concert T-shirt (thanks, Dad). She quickly ran her fingers through her hair and pulled it back into a half ponytail, half bun. She pocketed her Burt's Bees peppermint lip balm, grabbed her soccer bag, and slung it over her shoulder. She'd gotten a new combination, and left her books in her locker, making the executive decision that the first day of school was difficult enough without adding insult to injury by forcing herself to do homework.

She jumped down the stairs two at a time, rushing past her mother at the refrigerator and Krista, who was sitting at the kitchen table, nibbling on a whole-grain something or other.

"Honey?" her mom asked. "What would you like for breakfast?"

Charlie made a beeline for the back door. "Nothing. I'm good."

"You really should eat something," her mother encouraged. "You barely had dinner last night."

It was true. Charlie had been so tired from practice that she'd barely had the energy to lift the fork to her mouth.

Her eyes ticked over to her sister. She even hated the way Krista chewed. She took little tiny rabbit bites, as if she'd absorb less calories that way.

"Krista doesn't eat," she said dryly. "Why should I?"

Krista scowled up from her half-eaten bagel. "Get a life," she spat.

"Get a personality," Charlie shot back.

A honk came from the driveway.

"What was that?" Krista asked.

"That's the sound of me getting a life," Charlie retorted. She pulled the kitchen door open, then looked back over her shoulder. "Get used to it."

Charlie slammed the door in Krista's face and ran for the Town Car. She slid into the backseat. Much to her surprise, someone else was already sitting there.

"Hey." The girl smiled. Charlie recognized her from practice. She was the girl with killer triceps, who actually looked like a mini-Martie.

Carla slid in on the other side, and Charlie felt overwhelmed by the girl-bonding potential. It had been a long time since she'd had friends—now she was sandwiched between not one, but two potential new ones. The car started and rolled down Charlie's driveway.

"Charlie, this is Pickle," Carla introduced. "She's a freshman."

Pickle? Charlie reacted at the name but quickly masked her look of confusion. After all the comments thrown at her about *her* name, she wasn't about to ask.

"My real name's Nicole," Pickle offered. "When I was born, my sister was two. She couldn't say 'Nicole,' so . . ."

"She's Pickle," Carla chimed in. "I told her you'd be able to sympathize."

"Yeah," Charlie agreed. "I'm—"

"Charlie Brown," Pickle interrupted. "I heard." She shook her head. "Sucks."

"*You* could go by Nicole, you know," Charlie said bluntly, unsure why anyone would keep a name like Pickle if they had another, perfectly acceptable name to use.

Pickle shrugged. "Pickle's just who I am. Changing that would be changing *me*."

Charlie stared at Pickle. Changing herself was exactly what she wanted to do.

The car turned off Charlie's road and onto the Pacific Coast Highway. Carla and Pickle seemed mesmerized by the ridiculously huge houses built right into the cliffs.

"Man," Carla gasped. "Can you imagine being this rich?"

Charlie looked up at the homes she'd seen a million times. "Yeah, well, money doesn't buy happiness," she pointed out.

Pickle raised her eyebrows and looked at Charlie. "Maybe not happiness. But it buys a lot of other things."

Charlie smiled and sat back in her seat. *No amount of money buys you friends,* she thought. That was something you had to earn. And Charlie didn't want to get ahead of herself, but she couldn't help but hope that maybe, just maybe, she was on her way to earning some.

Her hunch proved right a few hours later in the cafeteria. Charlie was in her usual place—at the table in the far corner of the cafeteria, the smelly corner, near the trash room—when Carla and Pickle approached. Charlie looked up from her peanut-butter-and-honey sandwich, surprised.

"Are these seats taken?" Carla asked.

"Yeah, sorry," Charlie answered sarcastically. "Ten of my closest friends are joining me."

Pickle started to turn away. "Oh. Well, we can find somewhere else to—"

Charlie looked across the cafeteria at Regan laughing with her new friends.

What was that phrase her mother always used? The one about catching more flies with honey . . . ?

Charlie turned back to Carla and Pickle. "I'm kidding.

Of course they're free. Didn't you get the memo? I'm a social pariah."

"A piranha?" Pickle looked confused, her tray hovering inches from the table. "Just tell me, can I sit down or what?"

Charlie and Carla both laughed.

"Sure," Charlie said. "Have a seat." She smiled and took in the faces of her new friends. If Pickle and Carla thought she was cool enough to sit with, she might as well enjoy it.

Charlie glanced over at Regan.

She might as well enjoy it while it lasted.

Krista showed up at the beach promptly at three, ready for day one of hell week. She kept telling herself not to be nervous, but her fears, worries, and insecurities were getting to her. What if she didn't make the team? She'd be a bigger loser than Charlie already was, and Yale wouldn't even think about taking her.

Brooks, on the other hand, couldn't have cared less about tryouts. For her, it was all about Noah. She'd actually cut out of seventh period to primp in the school bathroom before practice. With her hair swept up and makeup perfect, she looked more like she was going to a movie premiere than a soccer practice. Only her tiny pink velour Juicy shorts and a white sports bra indicated otherwise.

Brooks pulled up right behind Krista and hopped out of her car. She spotted Noah right away.

"Is it possible that Europe made him even hotter?" Brooks mused, leaning in to Krista's window.

Krista glanced over at Noah. Brooks was right. He *had* gotten cuter. His piercing blue eyes and toned-but-not-to-the-point-of-obnoxious body already made girls look twice. But now, his sandy brown hair had grown out a little, and while he still gave off a preppy soccer vibe, he looked a little more relaxed and laid-back. Like he had chronic bed head or, more likely, was trying to shake off that Malibu trust fund image.

Traveling the world had obviously changed him, but underneath the messy rock star hair, he was still the same guy—Adidas flip-flops, Nike shorts, Urban Outfitters T-shirt, and—

Krista's gaze stopped abruptly on the clipboard in Noah's hand. The very sight of it made her stomach twist. She didn't like the idea of Noah and Martie evaluating her every move, especially when she, more than any recruit, deserved to be here. She made up her mind then and there. The new coaches needed to know that *she* was the star.

She slammed her car door shut and took a deep breath. It was now or never.

The girls were assembling down on the beach, some talking and laughing about school that day, others stretching quietly off to one side. Krista spotted Charlie right away, sitting between two other girls. She knew one girl was Carla, and she swore she heard Carla call the other girl "Pickle," but that couldn't possibly be right.

Sure, Gwyneth Paltrow had named her baby "Apple," but *Pickle?* That was like naming your kid "Asparagus" or "Cucumber."

It was more than not right. It was just . . . wrong.

Noah put down his clipboard. "Okay, everyone." He clapped and rubbed his hands together in anticipation. "We'll do a ten-minute warm-up jog down the beach, then come back and stretch." He clicked a button on his sports watch, setting the timer. "Ready?"

The girls jumped up, anxious to begin and eager to please. They knew Martie was watching. Krista felt a wave of relief wash over her. A simple warm-up jog was a great way to build confidence. She was a fast runner.

"Go!" Noah yelled. He clicked the watch again and took off down the beach, running on the wet sand right at the edge of the water. The girls followed, finagling for a prime spot. No one wanted to be last. Brooks and Krista ran easily at the front of the pack—Brooks determined to keep up with Noah, Krista determined to stay ahead of Charlie.

As she ran, Krista felt untouchable. There was a lightness to her stride that made her feel almost like she was flying. Noah kept the pace steady, not too fast but certainly not slow. Except for the slightest limp, he didn't look like he was recovering from an injury. Krista didn't have to push herself much to keep at the head of the pack.

After five minutes, Noah looped around and they headed south again. When Krista turned, she saw that Charlie wasn't far behind her. A few strides later, she was right next to her! Before Krista had a chance to change her gait, Charlie had flown past her, positioning herself right behind Noah.

Krista ran harder, pumping her arms, lengthening her strides. She pulled up even to Charlie and gave her a look of disgust.

"News flash," Krista said, annoyed. "This is a warm-up run, not a race."

Charlie ran harder, pulling even with Noah. Krista couldn't believe her sister! Was Charlie so pathetic that she was actually trying to make a ten-minute warm-up into serious competition? She pushed even more, ignoring the cramp starting to form in her left side. She passed Charlie and Noah, sprinting into the lead. Her little sister had nothing on her.

But suddenly, there was Charlie again. Right next to her. They were so close, their elbows were practically touching. Krista poured on the heat, and it became an all-out sprint to the finish, the two of them running as hard and fast as they possibly could, elbowing each other out of the way. Krista noticed Martie watching them curiously.

She was determined that Martie would see her worth. And she wouldn't seem worthy of anything if she let her non-soccer-playing sister beat her.

Krista ran even harder, sweat dripping into her eyes. Her legs pumped so fast, her heels were practically hitting her butt. One more push to seal her win and—wait, something didn't feel right. Krista glanced over her shoulder and saw that Charlie was walking. She'd bailed out. Not because she didn't have it in her, Krista knew, but to make her look foolish. To be a total brat.

Krista glared at her sister, who had stopped now and was laughing with Carla at her expense. Krista slowed to a walk and, drained of all energy, collapsed on the beach. Her mind was racing so fast that she couldn't form a coherent thought other than: *Must. Kill. Sister.*

Martie approached, kneeling down next to her. "You know this was a warm-up, not a race, right?" she asked, the admonishment evident in her voice.

Krista's heart, which was pumping so hard it felt like it was about to jump out of her chest, sank. Martie didn't get it. Charlie was competing with her, not the other way around. *Charlie* was the one who'd made it a race, who'd made it personal, who'd intentionally made her look foolish. Krista turned her head sideways. Charlie was leaning over with her hands on her knees, catching her breath. She gave Krista a big, fake smile.

"Nice run," she said smugly.

Krista clenched her jaw, fighting the urge to wring her sister's neck.

"Okay, everyone," Noah said as the last stragglers slowed to a walk. "Let's stretch, then we'll hit the dunes." Krista looked over at the huge sand dunes on the other side of the Pacific Coast Highway. *Please, God, no,* she thought. She'd just spent every last ounce of energy beating Charlie in the warm-up run; now she was going to have to beat her on the sand dunes too?

Fifteen minutes later, Noah had divided the girls into two groups, Krista in one and Charlie in the other. Charlie was in the first group with one of the seniors, Julie; the track girls, Heather and Karen; Pickle; and Brooks, who appeared to be permanently affixed to Noah's side. Noah pretended not to notice Brooks's gawking while he explained the first drill. Each group had to go up and down the dunes ten times. The last person from each group had to run the dunes an additional two times as punishment. Charlie eyed the dunes fearlessly. No problem. She wasn't about to be last.

Charlie's group lined up. Noah blew the whistle, and they were off. Charlie raced up the dunes to the blue-and-yellow flag on top. Running on the dry sand was difficult, her New Balances sinking into the ground. As she raced down, she had to slow herself or risk tumbling headfirst down the dune . . . which actually didn't seem like a bad idea.

pretty
TOUGH

At the bottom of the dune, one of the track girls, Heather, caught up with her and passed her on their second trip up. Karen, the other track star, was right on her heels—the three girls together were leading the pack as group two watched with dread, knowing they were up next. Charlie pushed up the second hill, getting to the flag second this time. By her fourth trip down, she could see Brooks and Pickle struggling in the back, battling it out for last place.

"Come on, Pickle," Charlie managed to exhale. Her chest was burning. It was getting harder and harder to breathe. Pickle didn't have enough energy to react but managed to pick up the pace a little, pushing her way to the flag.

On trip five, Charlie lost her balance, tripped, and literally rolled all the way down the dune. She could hear Krista and the other girls laughing.

"Oh my God." Krista groaned. "How embarrassing."

"Are you sure you two are related?" Buffi asked.

For being named Buffi, Charlie thought, Buffi was one of the least Buffi-ish girls ever. Instead of being a prissy party girl, she was a hard-core athlete. Buffi played soccer *and* softball and was in the top ten of her class. Even so, as one of Krista's best friends, Charlie was predisposed to hate her.

Krista rolled her eyes. "Tell me about it."

Charlie considered forgoing the other five trips up

the dunes and using her remaining energy to pummel Krista. Luckily, rational thought took over. She brushed the sand from her eyes and mouth and sprinted back up for trip six.

On her last trip up, Heather, Karen, and Julie were all ahead of her, sprinting down to the finish. Charlie knew she'd be fourth, which, considering her massive wipeout, wasn't horrible. What she didn't expect was that Brooks and Pickle would be dead even on their final trip up. Both girls were struggling.

Krista started cheering loudly for Brooks. "Beat her, Missy! You can do it!"

Other girls joined in, encouraging Brooks as if Pickle were invisible.

Charlie shot Krista a death stare. Here was Pickle, a stranger in a strange land, a freshman and total newcomer with a weird name, probably feeling scared and alone . . . and Krista was cheering for Brooks—stupid, vapid Brooks who clearly was only there to get Noah to like her.

"Let's go, Pickle!" Charlie screamed encouragingly, even though she was gasping for air. "You've got this!"

Carla, who was already lined up in group two, chimed in. "Yeah, Pickle!" she yelled. "You can do it!"

By the time Brooks and Pickle were racing down the dune, everyone was screaming and cheering. And when Brooks edged out Pickle by a tiny margin, Charlie's eyes filled with tears on Pickle's behalf. In the skirmish between good and evil, evil had won. Charlie watched Krista celebrating with Brooks.

"Oh my God," Krista gushed, putting her arm about her friend. "I knew you'd beat her." Buffi and Julie crowded around, high fiving Brooks.

"Who knew that girl would be so fast?" remarked Julie.

Brooks rolled her eyes. "Seriously. Now maybe she'll hurry back to wherever she came from."

Martie, who was standing near the second group, snapped up her head, reacting to Brooks's comment.

"Brooks," she ordered. "Get into the second group."

"Excuse me?" Brooks said.

"For a comment like that, you're running again. Or you can go home."

"What?" Brooks's jaw dropped in disbelief. "TNF!"

Charlie had no idea what "TNF" stood for, but whatever it was, it couldn't be good. Maybe now Brooks would leave . . . but Charlie had no such luck.

"Fine." Brooks shrugged. She lined up in the second group, behind Carla.

As Pickle ran her last trip up to the top and back alone, Charlie couldn't help but look at Martie and smile. Krista and Brooks might have won one battle, but with Martie's help, Charlie and the other outcasts were going to win the war.

After all, in the end, good always won out over evil, right?

• • •

After a quick water break and, at Noah's insistence, a banana to refuel, Martie took over the practice. The next hour was devoted to soccer drills and calisthenics. Krista liked this part because she was good at it and because she was determined to prove herself to Martie, who suddenly seemed to be watching everyone *but* her.

The next hour consisted of various touches on the ball—they'd travel down the beach kicking it and catching it, kneeing it and catching it, heading it and catching it—and between each drill the hopefuls would do forty-five seconds of push-ups, tuck jumps, crunches, mountain climbers, and anything else Martie could come up with. They ran and dribbled between cones all while being timed. The day finished with a game of keep-away on the beach. After twenty straight minutes of running around and chasing and passing the ball, Martie blew her whistle.

"Thank God." Brooks groaned. Legitimately out of breath, she also exaggerated her chest rising and falling for Noah's benefit. Krista stole a look the assistant coach's way and realized he *was* watching them.

Then suddenly, he winked. Krista glanced over her shoulder to see if Brooks caught it, but she had already turned away. Krista looked up quickly, but Noah was already conferring about something with Martie.

Had Noah Riley really just *winked?* Who winked anymore? It seemed retro—like leg warmers and jelly bracelets. But more important, who was he winking at? Brooks? Or her?

Before Krista could process a guess, Martie began another speech.

"Okay, everyone. I have one last thing for you to do before we call it a day." Groans rippled throughout the group.

"I want everyone on their feet," Martie said sternly. "Now!"

Krista mustered her strength and pushed herself up. Her body was so exhausted she felt like she could fall asleep standing up. She noticed the sun sinking lower toward the ocean. It was already six o'clock.

"On the count of three, everyone follow me," Martie explained. "One . . . two . . . *three!*" She whipped off her Adidas shirt, Brandi Chastain–style, kicked off her flip-flops, and made a beeline straight for the water. The entire team followed and plunged into the ocean, laughing and splashing each other.

Noah jumped up just as a wave was coming in and dove over it, landing right near Krista. He popped his head out.

"Hey," he said.

"Hey there," Krista responded.

"Nice work today," Noah complimented her. "You have definite skills."

"Thanks." Krista smiled. At least *someone* was watching.

Noah grinned, and in that moment Krista could see why Brooks had a thing for him. It was, undeniably, a killer smile. His teeth were straight and white, and his eyes crinkled a little around the corners.

"Brrr!" Noah shivered dramatically. "This water is colder than it looks!"

Krista laughed. "Don't be a baby. It's warm in this spot."

"Oh." Noah shrugged. "That's because I peed there."

A look of absolute horror crossed Krista's face. "What?"

Noah shook out his wet hair, laughing. "Dude, if you wanna make this team, you're going to have to learn how to take a joke."

Krista glared at him. That wasn't funny. There were no *ifs* about it. She *was* making this team. She had to.

Later that night, Krista sat at the kitchen table, listless, staring at her plate as if she was in a trance.

"Are you going to eat or not?" her dad asked. With her mom at a late meeting, he did what he did best—ordered a large pizza and Caesar salad from Vinnie's down the street. Half the pizza was already eaten, and Krista hadn't had one bite. She was too tired to open her mouth. Or chew. Or swallow.

"I'm sorry," she responded to her dad. Her eyelids felt so heavy. She could barely keep them open. It was all she could do to resist the urge to lay her head down on the table.

"So," her dad said, wiping his mouth with a paper towel that served as a napkin. "Tell me about practice. How was it? First day back and all."

Charlie perked up instantly. "Practice was great," she gushed, acting overly bubbly and strange. "But oh my God, this one girl today made the biggest fool out of herself."

"What happened?" Dad asked.

"She tried to race me on the warm-up run." Charlie laughed. "Can you believe that?"

Even with half-closed eyes, Krista could still muster a hard stare. Charlie shook her head, overacting. "It was *really* pathetic."

Her dad took a sip of his Coke. "Sounds like this girl was threatened by you."

"You think?" Charlie questioned, as if the thought had never occurred to her.

Krista got up from the table. She was far too tired to deal with Charlie's juvenile behavior. "I'm going to bed," she mumbled sleepily.

"Kris, I thought we were going to look at your college essays tonight—" her dad began. "You can't get into Yale on soccer alone. . . ."

"Maybe tomorrow." Krista groaned.

Right now, she didn't care about her college essays.

The only thing she wanted to look at was the inside of her eyelids.

The next day's practice was on the campus of Pepperdine University, which sat on a huge hill overlooking all of Malibu and the Pacific Ocean. The team wasn't required to ride from Beachwood to Pepperdine in the school van, but it was an option for girls who didn't have cars of their own. Or for girls like Charlie, who wouldn't even consider asking their self-involved older sisters for a ride.

Crammed in a van with a bunch of strangers wasn't Charlie's definition of ideal, but with Carla and Pickle there, it made it the ride a little easier. Charlie felt less self-conscious, safer with her new friends around.

"What do you think we're going to have to do today?" Carla asked the group casually. When no one answered, Charlie felt embarrassed for Carla and was about to say something, but then a cute brunette sophomore, Erica, piped up from the back of the van.

"Hide from Martie and Noah—and all those bananas?" she offered, quiet enough that Noah, who was driving, wouldn't hear. All the girls giggled. A naturally happy person, Erica had a way of making everyone laugh.

"Too bad we're at Pepperdine," her friend Fran added disappointedly. "Swimming was my favorite part of yesterday."

"So why not go out for the swim team?" Pickle offered.

"No way." Another girl, E-beth (short for Elizabeth) laughed, nudging Fran. "Then how would *she* get to be best friends with Brooks Sheridan?"

Fran elbowed E-beth. "Shut up!"

Erica and E-beth burst into a fit of laughter. Charlie simply couldn't believe it. Would someone actually suffer through hell week just to be on the same team as Brooks Sheridan?

"My sister goes to Pepperdine," Jamie, a junior, offered. "And there's a killer five-mile run there—off the campus and into the neighborhood, past some of the crazy mansions. I bet that's what we're doing today."

Sure enough, Jamie was right.

The girls took off in a large pack with Noah in the lead, running a loop around the campus and then out the back entrance and into the neighborhood. Once again, the last girl to finish had to do an extra campus loop. This time, Charlie and Carla made sure Pickle kept up with them.

Karen and Heather once again came in first and second, respectively. A strong runner, Krista finished in a pack right behind them. Jamie, Buffi, and Jen were next, followed by Carla and Charlie. Pickle finished just a few seconds behind them. Brooks crossed the line with E-beth, Erica, and a handful of other girls. Darcy, the pigtailed freshman, tied with a cute redhead, Ruthie. Poor Fran, who just wanted to meet Brooks, was dead last. When Martie told her to run another campus loop, she had tears in her eyes.

Carla, Pickle, and Charlie were already heading to their bags for a water break when Carla turned around. "Can I run with Fran?" she asked Martie.

Martie was surprised. "Do you want to?"

Carla nodded. "Sure."

Martie smiled. "Be my guest."

Charlie watched as Carla took off, joining Fran. "That's weird," she commented.

Pickle looked up from retying her shoelaces. "What's weird?"

"Why would Carla want to run another loop if she doesn't have to?" she asked. It didn't make sense. Was Carla a goody-goody like Krista?

When Carla finally returned with Fran, she smiled at Charlie mischievously.

"What?" Charlie asked. Why was Carla acting like such a weirdo?

"Don't tell anyone—we hit the vending machine in the quad," she whispered.

Pickle's eyes widened, impressed. "You what?"

Carla reached in her pocket and pulled out a piece of candy. "Sour Patch Kid?" Charlie eyed the sugar-coated candy, and her stomach began growling. One piece and the sugar rush could easily get her through the rest of practice.

Both Pickle and Charlie popped one into their mouths and chewed quickly.

Noah blew the whistle, signifying the end of crunches. Martie called out that next they were going to work on ball juggling and would be divided into groups of four. The point of the game was to form a circle and keep the ball in the air for as long as possible, juggling it and passing it to your teammates.

Martie read the groups aloud. "Jen, Ruthie, Erica, and Pickle. Heather, Buffi, Carla, and Fran. Brooks, Krista, Jamie, and Charlie. Casey, Zaida—"

Charlie stopped listening. Out of all the groups, why did she have to be in one with *Krista?* The idea of struggling with the soccer ball in front of her created a Grand Canyon–sized pit in Charlie's stomach. She wished she'd actually played with that Hacky Sack she'd found in her Christmas stocking last year instead of giving it to Marley, the golden retriever next door, as a chew toy. Maybe then she'd have a chance of surviving this drill with a shred of dignity.

When it came to footwork, even she had to admit that Krista was great. Once, during the last thirty seconds of a game, she'd seen Krista dribble the ball around four defenders to score a goal.

"We'll go for fifteen minutes," Martie instructed. "The

group that juggles the longest gets to sit out the next drill—"

"What's next?" Brooks interrupted, wanting to know what she was playing for.

"Suicide sprints," Martie responded. Charlie groaned. Every group wanted to sit out *that* drill. Suicide sprints were the worst. Martie would make them start at the goal line, then run to the eighteen-yard box, then run back to the goal line, then run all the way to midfield, then all the way back to the start.

Then, when you just wanted to collapse, you had to go all the way to the eighteen on the other side of the field and then back. For the grand finale, you had to run the whole field. And you were racing the entire time.

Charlie was keeping score, and so far she had beaten Krista at every drill. She doubted she'd be as successful at ball juggling.

"Okay," Martie continued, "if the ball hits the ground, your group starts over from zero."

Charlie felt nervous; her palms were sweating along with every other part of her body. She was already exhausted from the long run and drills. When she was surfing and got tired, she could rest. When she was snow-boarding on the half-pipe at Big Bear and her legs felt like they were about to give out, she could hit the lodge for hot chocolate. No such luck here.

"I know you're tired," Martie said sympathetically.

"Doing this at the end, when you're tired, teaches you to execute even when your body wants to give up."

Charlie wasn't about to give up. Not until her name was on that roster. Being part of a team wasn't her thing. But she wanted to prove Krista wrong. And until that list went up and *Charlie Brown* was written on it, Charlie was going to ball juggle or do anything else it took to make it.

Noah blew the whistle, and the drill began. Ten minutes into it, Charlie wanted to take a swan dive off the nearest cliff.

"Charlie!" Krista yelled, totally exasperated. "Come on!"

As much as Charlie hated it, this time she had to admit Krista was right. She couldn't keep the ball in the air if her life depended on it. And they had to start over from scratch every time Charlie's foot came anywhere near the ball.

Krista's frustration was quickly reaching a boiling point. "Okay," she told the others, "let's try not giving the ball to Charlie—"

"Hey! You can't just ignore me," Charlie insisted. "It's not fair!"

Even if Krista *was* better at ball juggling, her self-righteous superiority was impossible to swallow. Didn't the other girls notice what a witch she was?

Brooks slapped her back. "Life's not fair, kid. Get used to it."

Kid? Charlie felt like punching Brooks in the face. Maybe she'd be doing her a favor. Then she could get that second nose job she'd been telling Krista she wanted.

Krista kicked the ball to Brooks, who managed to juggle it three times before passing it on to Jamie. Then back to Krista. Then back to Jamie. Fifteen seconds were down. Back to Brooks, then Krista. Then Brooks, then Jamie. Thirty seconds. Back to Krista again.

"Charlie, get your foot on that ball," Martie instructed. She'd obviously noticed that Charlie wasn't participating.

Charlie threw her hands in the air, frustrated. "I'm trying, but Krista won't—"

"Krista," Noah called out, "you've got to pass."

She effortlessly and easily tapped the ball in Charlie's direction. "Here. Crybaby." Charlie made contact with the inside of her right foot, but before she could even blink, the ball was on the ground again.

The whistle blew. The drill was up. And their team had lost.

"Nice job," Krista sneered at Charlie, aggravated.

Noah slapped Charlie's back, then pulled her into a hug. "Don't worry. It just takes practice. We'll make sure you get it, okay?"

Charlie smiled, touched by Noah's attention. She turned away and noticed the winning team—Carla's—hugging and high fiving each other.

Charlie frowned. How was it that girls who were

strangers two days ago could already seem like best friends, while she and Krista—who'd known each other for fifteen years—couldn't get along if their lives depended on it?

When Krista got out of bed on Saturday morning, she was psyched. Today was the final day of hell week and by Monday morning, a list would be posted with the names of the girls who'd made the cut. Every muscle in her body ached, but it would be worth it when she saw *Krista Brown* on the list. She knew it would be there. It *had* to be there. It was too late to get on a club team for the fall, and if she wasn't playing, colleges might wonder what happened. She'd have to fake an injury. Maybe she could fall down the stairs. . . .

She and Charlie drove down to Zuma without a word exchanged between them. Krista thought of making small talk. She could have talked about how nice the other girls were or asked what Charlie thought their chances were of making it to states this year. She could have told Charlie that she played really aggressively as stopper in yesterday's scrimmage or admitted she was impressed with how ferocious Charlie was with the ball. But she didn't. What was the point? All her sister would do was throw some sarcastic remark her way. And Krista didn't need the attitude.

Instead, she just cranked up the new Killers album and sipped her nonfat, no-foam latte from Coffee Bean. She loved Coffee Bean. Did they have them on the East

Coast? The Ivys weren't quite as enticing without Coffee Bean. Then again, being with Cam would more than make up for it.

Cam . . . he was the reason she needed a coffee fix this morning. She was exhausted from staying up much too late with him. They had been hanging out in his parents' basement, which came complete with a pool table, PS2, and fifty-inch Panasonic flat screen mounted on the wall.

They pretended to watch a movie. But even after two hours, Cam refused to let her go.

"Not this time," he said between kisses. "Hell week has taken up all your attention. Now it's my turn."

Everything was all right—just blissful, in fact—until Cam decided he needed to talk. "Kris, have you thought about what I said in the closet the other day?"

Krista gazed at him. "What did you say?"

"You know, about owing me." Cam smiled playfully.

Krista giggled. "What, exactly, do you think I owe you?"

"I've been thinking," Cam said, holding her, suddenly serious. "We've been going out for a long time. And you know how I feel about you."

"Sure . . ." Krista said, intrigued.

"You've been so busy lately, and I was thinking. I missed you." He paused. "I think maybe . . . maybe it's time to take things to the next level."

Cam's eyes searched hers, looking for an answer.

Krista knew what he was talking about. "The next level" could mean only one thing—sex. She bit her lip.

This wasn't the first time it had come up. Cam told her that the guys on the team teased him about not "doing it." But he had been patient and defended her, insisting that they'd get to it when the time was right.

Krista knew she wasn't a prude—and she wasn't against the idea in general. She always told herself she would wait until she was in love and absolutely sure.

Now here she was—in love with Cam and absolutely sure of it.

"I'll think about it," she told him with a grin.

At that moment, it seemed to be enough for Cam. They kissed some more. Then, at midnight, he let her go.

Krista hardly slept that night, thinking about Cam's question. But she couldn't dwell on how tired she was now. This was her last day to prove herself. And even if she had to drink eight lattes and five Red Bulls, she was going to get herself amped up enough to do it.

When she and Charlie arrived at the beach, Noah told the girls that he and Martie had a treat in store for them.

"Let me guess," Erica offered. "Bananas for everyone?"

Daily banana breaks were now a running joke on the team. Maybe the girls were so exhausted that anything would make them laugh. Still, just the word *banana* had taken on a special silliness.

Martie laughed at Erica's joke, then told them practice was going to be a little different today and much more fun.

"Thank God." Brooks sighed. She'd been complaining the whole week about how much "this soccer thing" sucked, especially since she'd made no progress with Noah.

"He must be gay," she'd determined at lunch yesterday afternoon. "That's the only explanation."

Martie clapped and the girls started moving. First they stretched, took off their shoes, and went for a long run in the wet sand for resistance training. Next were calisthenics, where each girl got to choose one exercise.

"Jumping jacks!" Buffi called out.

"Push-ups," Jen suggested.

"Dead mans," Erica offered.

Martie looked confused. "Dead mans?"

"Like, if conditioning's not over soon, I'm going to be dead, man." All the girls cracked up. Martie laughed and blew her whistle.

After a water break, Martie announced they'd practice headers in the water.

Internally, Krista winced. She'd torn her ligament going for a header. Since then, she avoided them whenever possible.

Martie divided everyone into twos based on where they were standing. Krista, at the end, was the only one left partnerless.

"I'll pair up with her," Noah offered.

Great, Krista thought. She couldn't have asked for a worse partner. If anyone could spot a player masking an injury, it would be Noah Riley.

Still, she smiled appreciatively and avoided eye contact with Brooks. Without even looking, Krista could feel her jealous stare.

"Ready?" Noah smiled at Krista.

"Almost." She took her hair out of her long blond ponytail and flipped her head over. She gathered her hair again and twisted it into a high bun on the top of her head.

"Whoa," Noah whispered, his eyes wide.

"What?" Krista asked. She glanced around in the surf. Was there a jellyfish nearby?

"No." Noah shook his head. "It's nothing, nothing. You ready now?"

"S-sure." Krista grinned through her fears.

Noah threw the ball in her direction. She gritted her teeth and headed it back to him. He got under it and headed it to her right, making it tough to return. She ran into the surf but couldn't quite get it. Maybe if she dove—

Her brain flashed back to that day last season, the feel of her ligament snapping, the pain.

No. She couldn't chance it.

She leaned forward. Her forehead barely made contact

with the ball; she headed it down to Noah's feet right before she belly flopped into the surf. A wave crashed over her. She surfaced with a mouthful of sand.

A second later, Noah was at her side, pulling her up.

"You okay?" he asked. He searched her arms and legs, then her face for signs of injury.

Krista brushed her wet hair out of her eyes and looked right at him. She'd never noticed the little scar above Noah's left eyebrow before. It was nice. It really gave his face character.

"Yeah. Totally," she told him.

"Krista," Martie shouted. "A little hustle. Get under it next time!"

Krista frowned. Didn't Martie notice her sand snack? Didn't that count for anything?

"Don't worry about her," Noah muttered. "She's tough on everybody. Including herself."

Krista smiled, grateful for the encouragement.

Practice ended with four-versus-four games in the wet sand and surf. Because there wasn't an even number, Martie and Noah played against Jamie, Krista, Fran, and Casey, an incredible kicker who had just moved from the East Coast. The girls still managed to lose with twice as many players. Martie effortlessly trapped, dribbled, headed the ball. She seemed to pass to Noah more out of obligation than necessity. She could practically take on all four of them at once. After Martie shot the ball past Jamie, she blew the whistle. It was time for a swim in the ocean. Krista led as the girls sprinted for the water and dove in.

After a few minutes, Krista made her way back to the beach. There, something amazing caught her eye. "You guys," she yelled. "Look!"

Buffi, Julie, and Brooks looked up. "The In-n-Out truck!" they screamed in unison.

Martie smiled. "Congratulations, everyone. This is my treat for surviving hell week. Whether your name is on the list or not Monday, you all are amazing athletes and young women. Now get your In-n-Out before it gets cold." The girls rushed the truck, ecstatic.

In-n-Out Burger was a California delicacy. They made the best fast-food burgers in the whole world and had a secret menu that only "In-n-Outsiders" knew about. For instance, even though it wasn't on the menu, you could order triple-triples after ten o'clock at night, or you could ask for your burgers "animal style" and get grilled onions, pickles, extra sauce, and special mustard flavoring for the meat patty. Krista's mouth was watering at the thought. She wondered how many burgers she could cram into her belly before—

"Don't even think about it," Brooks reprimanded. "Do you know how many calories are in those things?" Krista hung back in the line but watched as Noah ordered a double-double dripping in all kinds of high-calorie good-ness. He took a huge bite and looked at Krista, who was clearly hesitating.

"You're missing out," he said, his mouth full. Krista debated. How many crunches would it take before bedtime to work off a double-double? One thousand? Ten thousand? There was an *I Love the 90s* marathon on VH1 tonight. She could watch while she crunched, although it would probably take from 1990 to 1993 to burn off a double-double.

"Does anyone want to split a burger?" Krista asked aloud. Buffi, Zaida, and Heather looked at her like she was an insane person as they ordered burgers, fries, and milk shakes. No one wanted to share.

"Here," Noah offered. "I will." He walked over and offered his burger. "Wanna bite?"

Krista's stomach fluttered at the invitation. He was just offering a bit of his burger. So why did it seem like . . . more?

Brooks glared at Krista. "It's going to go straight to your soccer thighs," she remarked, hitting Krista where she was most insecure.

Krista bit her lip. She shook her head. "No thanks. I'm good."

"You *sure?*" Noah said, waving the burger under her nose. His eyes sparkled mischievously.

Krista recoiled under Brooks's watchful glare. "Yeah, I'm . . . um . . . not interested," she answered sharply. "*Really.*"

Noah frowned. "Fine. Suit yourself."

As he walked back toward the truck, Krista turned around, staring out at the water.

Why did she suddenly feel guilty? She had a boyfriend she was crazy about. But the way Brooks was staring at her . . . it was as if she'd done something wrong. She suddenly felt like the world's biggest jerk.

She felt like an even bigger one when she heard Brooks run after Noah, saying that *she'd* have a bite of his double-double instead.

"Did we make it?" Pickle asked as she and Carla scanned the list posted on Martie's door for their names. Charlie watched from a bench across the hall. She'd look when there were less people. Everyone was crowded around, elbowing each other, straining to see the list. Brooks had already digested the news that she'd suffered through hell week for nothing. No Noah and no place on the team.

"Whatever," Charlie heard Brooks say. "Even if he wasn't gay, Noah Riley is so two years ago." She walked off, acting like she didn't care.

Charlie wished she could be so casual. But her name *had* to be on the list. She wanted it so much.

Charlie watched as other freshmen and sophomores stared at the list, wide-eyed. Darcy and Ruthie found their names, but Casey and Fran had failed to make the team. E-beth threw an arm around Fran, comforting her, despite her own disappointment in not making the team. Darcy and Ruthie waited to celebrate until the other girls had gone—either to their next class or into the girls' bathroom to cry in private.

Charlie watched Pickle and Carla anxiously. Without hearing what they were saying, she could instantly tell what had happened: Pickle's shoulders rounded and her head hung low. Carla gave her a hug, which only made it worse. Unable to hold her emotions back, Pickle began to cry.

Carla had made the team; Pickle hadn't.

Charlie didn't know what to do. Pickle was her friend and a great goalie. She was also an awesome outside back. But the team already had more than enough defenders. Darcy was a better goalie, and Zaida was both an incredible goalie *and* a strong forward.

Had Pickle tried out any other year, she would have made the team easily. This year, one goalie had to be cut. Pickle was the obvious choice.

Charlie knew she had to say something. She moved toward Pickle and Carla—and bumped shoulders with someone.

Regan Holder—accompanied, of course, by her ever-present posse of airhead girl-bots.

Regan looked Charlie over, then glanced at Pickle and Carla. "I see you have some new friends," she taunted. "Do they—*know about you?*"

"Shut up, Regan," Charlie muttered, clenching her fists.

"Or, wait. I know! They're already *on your team*, right?" She laughed haughtily. The airheads joined in.

Charlie gritted her teeth. "Leave them out of this."

"Fine, fine." Regan put up her hands in surrender. "But they're new. How long do you think it will be till they find out about you, *Charlie Brown?*"

Regan smirked and sauntered off down the hall. Charlie watched her go, then approached her friends.

"Who was that?" Carla asked, staring after the popular girls.

"No one," Charlie muttered. "Don't worry about them." She turned to Pickle, took in her tear-streaked face. "I'm sorry, Pickle," she said. "You should have made it."

Pickle nodded and grabbed her backpack. "I'm going to be late for World Civ," she said softly. She slung her pack over her shoulder and disappeared into the sea of students making their way to class.

A pit formed in Charlie's stomach on Pickle's behalf. After riding to school with her every day and surviving hell week together, she knew how badly Pickle wanted on the team. And she had wanted it for the right reasons.

Carla nudged Charlie with her elbow. "What?" she asked, snapping back to reality.

"Did you see? Your name's the first one on the list."

Charlie looked up—squinted.

Charlie Brown.

Oh my God. Carla was right. It really was up there. *Her* name in all its ridiculousness was actually up there. *First.*

"We made it," Carla said, sounding as shocked as Charlie felt. "Do you know what this means . . . ?"

Charlie stared at her name, unable to peel her eyes away. She knew exactly what it meant: she was on the team.

Krista wormed her way through the crowd of ecstatic or crushed hopefuls and gasped when she saw the list.

"You've got to be kidding me." Krista spun around to face Charlie. "I can't believe you made it."

Charlie plastered on a fake smile. "Woo! Go, B-dub!" she said, overly enthusiastic.

Krista folded her arms in front of her chest. "Well, congratulations. You've proven your point. Now you can crawl back under whatever lifeguard station you hang out at and leave the team to the people who care."

Actually, that had been exactly the plan, Charlie thought, but Krista would never know it. Because in that moment, Charlie made up her mind.

"You know what I'd rather do?" She moved closer so that she was right in Krista's face. "Play soccer."

Despite joining the team out of pure spite, now **six** that Charlie was a full-fledged member of the Beachwood girls' soccer team, even she had to admit it was one of the best decisions she'd ever made—for the totally wrong reason. After the first week of official practice, Charlie was happier than she had ever been. It was becoming glaringly obvious to anyone in school which girls played soccer: they all had permanent shin guard tan lines. And for the first time, Charlie felt like a part of them. Like she had a group where she belonged.

She and Carla had three of the same classes together and often met up with Pickle in between. Lunch was spent at Charlie's cafeteria table or on the grass in the quad. Some days Jen and Jamie ate with them. There was a freshman boy named Benji who Pickle constantly bantered with. Benji had taken a definite liking to Pickle and was always hanging around, cracking jokes and being the resident goofball. And although Charlie was hesitant to trust anyone after being so burned by Regan, she couldn't help being excited about the turn of events in her life.

Her days of feeling like a high school nobody were fading into memory.

Today, Charlie and **Carla were** hurrying to the locker room because they were meeting up with Pickle to go to the next *Harry Potter* movie.

As she changed back into her school clothes, Charlie could hear Krista babbling endlessly about the party she was going to tonight.

"There could be over two hundred people there," Krista said breathlessly. "I think pretty much the whole school's going."

Charlie pictured a different time and place, some kind of alternate, parallel universe in which she and Krista got along—where instead of talking about a party in front of her as if she didn't even exist, Krista would turn to her and say, "Charlie? You're coming, right? To the party?"

Charlie would hesitate because she'd probably have *lots* of other plans, but Krista would insist. "You *have* to be there. It wouldn't be the same without you."

Charlie would agree to go. Krista would give her a ride, of course. They'd have the best time, and at the end of the night, when they knew they'd missed their curfew, they'd even sneak into the house together, making a pact not to let their parents find out.

They'd actually be like sisters for once instead of enemies.

But as she slipped her sweatshirt over her head and stuffed her sweaty soccer clothes into her duffel bag, she knew that conversation had about as much of a chance of happening as her becoming homecoming queen.

She rolled her eyes at her sister's chattering.

"Where're we meeting Pickle?" Carla asked.

Charlie grabbed her stuff. "Library. She was going to do homework until we finished."

Suddenly, Martie poked her head out of her office. "Charlie, Krista? Can I talk to you guys for a sec?"

Reluctantly, Charlie walked in behind Krista and took a seat. She wondered if she was in some kind of trouble. In practice today, she was going hard for the ball when she made a slide tackle and "accidentally" nailed Krista in the shin. Krista had yelped in pain and muttered something under her breath. Charlie didn't quite catch what it was.

"After today's scrimmage, I've made a decision," Martie explained. "Charlie, I'm moving you up to offense."

Charlie gasped. "What? *Offense?*"

She couldn't believe it. She'd always been a defender; she was a defender at heart. It fit her personality. Defenders, often overlooked and underappreciated, were the hardest workers on the team. They never got any of the glory. Fouls, slide tackles . . . they had to be tough, doing whatever it took to keep an opposing player from getting a shot on goal. They were blamed if the ball got through the defensive line but never praised. People only noticed when they screwed up.

And the hardest-working defender of all was the keeper.

"You want me to move to midfield?" Charlie asked. Maybe midfield wouldn't be so bad. It was at least better than—

"Actually," Martie interrupted, "I want to move you all the way up. To center forward."

"What?" exclaimed Charlie. "You want me to be . . ." She could barely say it. "A forward?" she whispered.

"What?" Krista echoed, horrified. "But center forward is my position. You can't give it to—"

"I don't want your stupid position!" Charlie interrupted.

Forwards were, by nature, glory hogs. Forwards got all the attention and praise. It was the forwards who people talked about after the game, the forwards who had their names printed in the paper. Which explained why Krista had been the forward of all forwards, the *center* forward, for three years running.

"Charlie, we need someone like you up there," Martie said encouragingly. "You're aggressive and tough. You don't back down. We have two weeks until our first game; I'm still playing around with the lineups. . . . Just give it a try, okay?"

Charlie nodded meekly. Could she argue? She wanted to be in the starting lineup. If this was the only way . . .

"What about *me?*" Krista asked. "Where am I supposed to go?"

Martie answered simply. "The team's old center mid, Morgan, graduated last year. There's no one strong enough to take her place—except you. I want you to try out there."

Krista perked up, surprised. "Really?"

Charlie shook her head, shocked. Unbelievable. Forwards had to rely on the center midfielder most of all. If she was center forward and Krista was center mid . . . ? One word came to mind: *di-saster.*

Charlie couldn't believe it. Krista might be a great player, blah blah blah, but she was literally the biggest baby on the field. Just today, she'd backed off from two headers that had clearly been hers, ones she might have even put inside the eighteen. The ball had been placed so perfectly that all she needed to do was stand there and it would have bounced off her perfect blond hair . . . but Krista had actually run away from it, leaving first Ruthie, then Heather to make crazy dives for the ball. Now Martie was, what? Rewarding her?

Charlie stared at her beaming sister and was disgusted. *Center mid.* The girl who played that position was usually the strongest, most technically skilled player on the team. She was the anchor of the offense, so the team's scoring potential and strategy began with her. Did Martie really think Krista was the best choice? What about Carla? Or Jamie? Or one of the lunch ladies in the cafeteria?

Charlie felt a strange sensation in the pit of her stomach.

She hoped it was just a reaction to the chicken nuggets she'd scarfed down at lunch but knew better. It was the thought of working so closely with Krista that was making her sick.

On Monday afternoon at practice, once all their drills were complete, Noah handed out red and yellow jerseys for a scrimmage. After he handed Krista a red one, Charlie waited, thinking, *Yellow, yellow, yellow. Please let me* not *be on Krista's team.*

But of course, Noah tossed a red one to her.

Her shoulders sagged and she glared at him. "Are you deaf?" she asked. "Didn't you hear me *thinking* yellow?"

Noah gave her a friendly slap on the back. "Put it on. It'll bring out your eyes." Charlie laughed and slipped the jersey over her head, her fate decided.

At least it was Noah who was dooming her, Charlie thought. Since the first day of practice, he had encouraged her more than anyone else. Charlie felt, even though it sounded silly, like they had a special bond.

As soon as the scrimmage began, Charlie knew she was going to hate this new arrangement. The sound of Krista's voice was grating on her as her constant chatter instructed Charlie what to do. *Turn inside, mark so-and-so, pass back . . .* It was like an endless phone conversation with Brooks—Krista never shut up!

And as the yellow jerseys scored against them not once but twice, Krista was becoming even more frustrated with the offense.

pretty
TOUGH

"Okay, you guys," she said. "We need to connect and score here."

Charlie rolled her eyes. "Oh, *that's* what we're supposed to be doing?" she asked sarcastically. "I thought we were just supposed to boss people around instead of going for the ball. You know, like you're doing."

Krista glared at Charlie. "Why don't you grow up?"

"Actually, I am," Charlie retorted. "At a rate of about an eighth of an inch a year."

"I am seriously going to kill you," Krista said through clenched teeth.

Charlie laughed. "I'd love to see you try." Martie blew the whistle. Charlie vowed that for the rest of the game, she would listen to Noah and Martie . . . and even Carla, who shouted instructions from the defensive line. The one voice she would tune out was Krista's. She did, and the red team went on to win three to zero.

It was the end of Krista's first full week of center mid. She sat in Cam's basement as he unbuttoned the top button on her white Abercrombie blouse.

"Cam, hold on," she said.

"What?" he asked. "What's wrong?"

Krista sighed and sank into the couch pillows. "I don't know. Sometimes it feels like everything."

"Everything?" He laughed. "What're you talking about? You're, like, what, in the top ten in our class? You're hot. And you just moved to the top spot on your team. Everyone knows you're the best player. . . ."

Not everyone, Krista thought. Martie and Noah barely gave her the time of day on the field—even in her new position. All Martie did was bark at her in the practices, and Krista was used to free-flowing praise.

Noah, on the other hand, seemed more occupied with Charlie than anyone else on the field. In his eyes, Krista felt, she might as well not even exist.

Moving to center mid *was* a victory. But with so little fanfare, it hadn't felt much like one.

"C'mon," Cam asked. "Half the people in school would kill to be you. What else do you want?"

Krista shrugged. Was it wrong that she wanted more? She wanted to be the team captain. She wanted to have no fear on the field. She also wanted Charlie off *her* team.

"It's just my sister," Krista explained. "She's a crazy person on the field. . . . I feel like I'm competing with her every time we go out there. She's always yelling at me for not going for the ball, which is totally untrue. Every time she speaks, I seriously feel like I'm going to go postal!"

"Kris—whatever," Cam said compassionately. "It's understandable that you'd be a little tentative."

"I'm not tentative!" she snapped defensively. "I just play smart. Is it so wrong that I don't want another ACL tear?"

"That's what I was just saying," Cam muttered.

For a moment, they sat in silence. After what Cam deemed to be an appropriate amount of time, he reached over and started kissing her neck.

Normally, Krista could lose herself in the feeling of it. But now, a million images flashed through her brain. Charlie on the field—brave and terrifying. Martie yelling orders. And Noah . . .

I can't do this, Krista thought. *Not right now.*

She stood up. "Cam, I'm sorry. Our first game's on Tuesday—I guess I'm just—I don't know, distracted."

Cam put up his hands, surrendering. "Fine, go."

Krista was hurt. "I—I don't want to leave. . . . I just wanted to talk."

Cam looked at her. "We've been doing that all night."

Krista searched Cam's handsome face. He was right. Most people would kill to be her—especially right now, when she was alone with Cam.

"Fine," she said, scooting toward him. "Then let's do something else." She planted a passionate kiss on his lips.

The next day, Martie gathered the team around after practice. It had been a long morning. While Noah had been cheering on Charlie and building her up, Martie wouldn't get off Krista's back.

"Krista!" she shouted. "Act, don't react. Let's go. Win those fifty-fifties."

"You're backing down," Martie yelled five minutes

later when Charlie beat Krista to the ball. "Be aggressive out there!"

Krista felt herself getting more and more frustrated with every word out of Martie's mouth. God, did this woman just hate her? And what about Noah? It was like he was adding insult to injury, keeping his attention focused squarely on Charlie.

"Good, Charlie," he called out when Charlie jumped for a header. Darcy blocked the shot. "Finish it now! Look for help! Ruthie—get in there."

Krista stopped and stared at Noah. Was she invisible? *She* could have gotten in there.

"Krista," Martie yelled, "this isn't a water break."

Krista resisted the urge to roll her eyes. She wished she could grab the spare ball that sat on the sidelines and punt it right at Martie. She wished Martie came with a mute button.

But at the end of practice, Martie was still all talk. When she told everyone that she had a few important announcements, Krista knew what was coming. Their first game was only days away. Martie was going to announce the starting lineup.

Charlie bit her lip nervously as the team gathered around Martie. Reactions were kept to a minimum because the girls who made it didn't want to rub it in anyone's face. And the truth was that one week you could be a starter and the next you could find yourself sitting on the bench for half the game. The lineup changed quickly because players' abilities and team dynamics were changing as well.

"Starting keeper," Martie called out, "Darcy Yankovich." Darcy, an adorable freshman and a ruthless goalie, beamed proudly. Carla put an arm around Darcy and gave her a half hug. Charlie was too nervous to even look up. She stared at a rock on the ground.

"Sweeper will be Jamie Bonter. Outside backs, Erica Hananel and Julie Theiser. Stopper, Carla Hernandez." Carla nodded and gave a half smile, trying to contain her excitement. The girl who played stopper was usually one of the strongest players on the team. It was her job to mark and block the best scorer on the opposing team. And although she was the first line of defense, she could at times come up and switch with the center midfielder, depending on the situation.

"Center mid, Krista Brown," continued Martie. Charlie could just picture the smug look on Krista's face.

"Right mid, Heather Edwards. Left mid, Buffi Long."

Charlie wrung her hands nervously, still staring at the ground. This was it. She felt like her stomach was making its way into her throat.

"Right wing, Jen Schwartzott. Left wing, Ruthie Merle."

Charlie's heart was pounding so loudly she was sure everyone else could hear it. "And striker . . ."

Charlie Brown, Charlie Brown, Charlie Brown, Charlie thought. It was the one and only time Charlie had ever wanted to hear her name called out.

"Charlie Brown!"

Everyone applauded. Charlie felt a wave of relief and pride crash over her. She'd made it into the starting lineup—as the team's starting striker! All the best players were in the midfield, and now she was one of them.

Finally, it was going to be her time in the spotlight. It was going to be her time to shine! She hadn't even realized how badly she'd wanted this until it had happened. This year was getting better and better. For once, Charlie couldn't wait to see what would happen next.

"Last," Martie said, "I'd like to announce the team captain." Team captain was always a senior, a girl who'd been on the team all four years . . . and although Krista had had to redshirt one season due to her ACL tear, she had technically been on the team the entire time. Charlie knew what was coming and was dreading it.

"It was a tough decision," Martie began. "Each and every one of you brings so much to this team. But one student has been a leader on and off the field. In the classroom, at practice, she exemplifies what it means to be a B-dub student. And that student is . . ."

Charlie watched Krista lift her head, ready to celebrate and relish her teammates' applause.

"Jamie Bonter," Martie announced.

Charlie was completely stunned.

Krista let out an audible gasp.

Jamie looked the most shocked of everyone as her teammates cheered and applauded.

Everyone loves Jamie, Charlie realized. She'd make a great captain—to everyone but Krista, who was now sulking in the corner.

Charlie walked over to Jamie and said, loud enough for Krista to hear, "Congratulations. It couldn't have happened to a more deserving person." When Charlie looked around for her sister, she was already gone.

seven

The week of their first game, which would be against Curtis High, Charlie sat at the desk in her room, cramming for her test on *To Kill a Mockingbird*. Martie, whom she had to call "Miss Reese" during class, had assigned it weeks ago, and Charlie still had only read the first three chapters.

Carla had finished the book in three days and actually read it a second time because she loved it so much.

Charlie tried to focus. The test was tomorrow, so she would have to resort to online Cliffs Notes if she didn't finish it. But every time she tried to concentrate on Scout and Jem and all the other characters with bizarre names, her mind wandered . . . to every possible shooting drill she'd done and every possible way she could nudge the ball into the goal.

Through their one shared wall, Charlie could hear Krista on her cell phone with Brooks, bitching, of course. For someone who had a pretty perfect life, Krista found a lot to complain about. It sounded like she was stressed about Cam—something he had asked her to do—but

Charlie couldn't figure out what. She pressed her ear against the wall, listening for a scoop . . . or at least something to blackmail Krista with later.

"I know everyone has"—Krista's voice came through muffled—"but why is he suddenly talking about this now? It doesn't make sense, Missy. Cam's always been happy with the way things were."

Charlie pressed closer, attempting to soak up every word.

RING! Charlie jumped at the sudden noise, then realized it was the house phone ringing in the hallway.

Moving away from the wall and back to her pretend studying, she figured it was probably Cam calling for Krista. When she tied up her cell phone, he sometimes resorted to calling the house.

Suddenly, there was a knock at her door.

"Charlie," her dad said, pushing open the door and handing her the cordless. "It's for you."

Charlie blinked. Before joining the soccer team, she never talked to anyone on the phone. She didn't even bother answering it because it was never for her. Now, between Carla and Pickle, the home phone was ringing for Charlie at least two or three times a night. She still wasn't used to it.

"Hello?" she asked into the receiver.

"Oh my God. I'm so nervous for the game," Carla said. "Are you?"

Charlie felt a wave of relief. She wasn't alone. "I'm trying to read for tomorrow's test and all I can think about is how many different ways I can score off the goalpost this Friday."

For the next hour, Carla and Charlie talked about everything from the team's starting lineup to which boys in their class were cute (Charlie said nobody because they all were covered in zits. Carla said Nate, a tall sophomore with short, almost-shaved dark hair and great eyes who played goalie on the boys' soccer team).

Finally, Charlie admitted that she was in trouble. She hadn't read half the book, and she was going to fail tomorrow's test. She had to go.

Carla offered to help.

"Why do you think I called in the first place?" she teased.

Over the next hour, they went over the themes, characters, and plot from *To Kill a Mockingbird*. By ten o'clock, Charlie had taken copious notes. Then there was a knock at her door.

"Hold on," Charlie said into the phone. "Come in."

Her mom pushed the door open slightly. "Sweetheart, it's time to say good night." Charlie smiled mischievously. "Good night, Mom," she said.

Her mom raised an eyebrow. "Very funny, but you know full well what I meant, young lady. Tell Carla you have to go."

"Wait," Carla's voice came through the receiver. "Are you and Pickle still spending the night after the game?"

"Definitely," Charlie said. "We'll give Pickle the play-by-play of all the ways we kick Curtis's butt in the game."

"Great!" Carla cheered. "But first, you have to kick the butt of that test."

Krista was changing into her uniform when Charlie burst into the locker room, looking for Carla.

"Carla!" Charlie called out, knocking into Krista as she brushed past her.

"Watch it," Krista snapped, almost losing her balance.

Oblivious, Charlie held up a sheet of paper with one giant red letter on it.

"I got a B-plus!" she said, elated.

Krista moved to the mirror as Carla rushed over, wearing only one sock and shin guard. She enveloped Charlie in an enormous bear hug and squealed with delight. "I knew you could do it!"

In the mirror, Krista gave Charlie an odd look. Hugging? Squealing? Since when did her sister do either of those things?

Krista ignored Carla's excited chatter as she pulled her hair up into a bun. Staring at her reflection in her locker mirror wasn't vanity; it was routine. And she always had the exact same routine on game day.

First, she would lie in bed for five minutes staring at

her soccer wall. This was the wall directly across from her bed. There was a shelf on the wall that held her various soccer trophies and awards. Above the shelf hung a giant black-and-white poster of Mia Hamm. Under the shelf, she'd taped inspiring magazine covers and quotes, including the *Newsweek* cover of Brandi Chastain at the 1999 World Cup finals in Pasadena, where she had won the game for the team in a shoot-out.

Next to her World Cup shrine was a picture of Bethany Hamilton, the surfer from Hawaii whose arm had been partially bitten off by a shark. Most people didn't realize that Bethany wasn't only an amazing surfer, but also a skilled soccer player. Krista had found the article in one of Charlie's surf magazines and had ripped out the picture of Bethany, mid–slide tackle on the soccer field. Underneath, Krista had neatly printed a quote from Bethany, "In soccer you can score or succeed in the last minute." It reminded Krista to never give up.

Krista let her eyes wander around that wall, soaking up strength and inspiration. When she walked onto the field, she wanted to be the best. On the field she had permission to shine. It was the one place she felt free and uninhibited, not plagued by how she looked or what people thought of her. It was the one place she felt truly herself, and she was determined that everyone would see her best self possible.

When she was finally ready to leave her bedroom and

get ready, there was usually a card from her dad, propped up outside her bedroom door. The card wished her good luck or reminded her of something she needed to focus on or repeated a quote that her father found inspirational. Sometimes the cards were funny and made her laugh. And today was no different. Except that when Krista grabbed the envelope, something caught her eye: a second card, outside Charlie's bedroom door. Krista felt a pang of jealousy in her stomach. When it came to Charlie, even getting a card from their dad was competition.

On game day, classes were always excruciating to sit through. Krista doodled in the margins of her spiral notebooks, writing key phrases to herself. *Play hard. No fear.* Krista knew she had the habit of backing down sometimes. And if she hadn't known, she could always count on Charlie to point it out.

"What's wrong with you?" Charlie would yell. "Are you actually trying to avoid the ball? Do you want to actually play soccer? Or just talk to us while *we're* trying to play?"

Krista wished Dr. Payne would wire Charlie's jaw closed.

Besides, Charlie didn't get it. Krista had been in awful pain after her torn ligament. Pain like she had never known before.

So fine, maybe she wasn't always first to the ball, and yes, maybe she would slow down a little rather than plowing into someone like a crazy person—but so what? She played smart, with precision and accuracy, and she had a great sense of what was happening on the field. Charlie was too busy acting like she was the only person on the grass to see that.

As she doodled, she had to resist writing the other thoughts swimming around in her head. *I ate a Twix bar when Brooks wasn't looking. I'm not sure I'm ready to have sex with Cam. My thong is cutting off my circulation.*

Once school was over, Krista rushed to the locker room, avoiding any hallway where Cam might lurk. She couldn't be distracted by a tryst in the janitor's closet today. She had to be on the field early, with enough time to complete her warm-up routine.

As soon as she got to the locker room, she changed clothes.

Brooks always said with acting that it was important to look the part, and Krista agreed. With every deliberate action—pulling on her shorts, squeezing into her white sports bra, securing her shin guards, carefully tying her cleats—she felt stronger and more invincible. Slipping on her blue-and-yellow jersey (she was lucky number seven), it was as if she were putting on armor, preparing for battle. She always made sure to bring her lucky socks—the socks she was wearing when she had scored four goals in her club's league semifinals. Since then, she'd only had to play one time without her lucky socks. During that game, she'd played so badly her coach had actually benched her.

Once she was dressed, she would pull her hair up into a loose messy bun. She didn't like the bun to be too tight. She still wanted it to look pretty. Running around and sweating like a boy was no excuse to *look* like a boy. She finished off her look with a coat of strawberry lip gloss and a squirt of Miracle perfume (she didn't want to smell like a boy, either).

Next, she grabbed her Nano. Pre-iPod Krista used a CD Walkman, but since last Christmas, it had been the Nano exclusively. She scrolled to her "game day mix," which started with Eminem's "Lose Yourself." The song always got her going. And although the mix had mostly rap and hip-hop, she did include "Hero" (by the Foo Fighters, not Enrique or Mariah) for that final bit of inspiration.

Now she sat in a corner of the locker room, her head down. As she cranked up the volume, it was as if the music was pulsating through her body. She mouthed the lyrics to herself, managing to get through the entire first song before Martie entered the locker room.

"All right, everyone," she called out excitedly. "We ready?"

Krista took out her headphones and heard cheers go up around the room. The entire team seemed as fired up as she was.

They'd spent the entire month of September working hard, training hard, and playing hard. Everything in their lives revolved around soccer. "Salt and pepper" weren't spices: it was a passing drill. And "World Cup" wasn't a soccer tournament: it was an elimination game they played at the end of particularly good practices. Now it was time for their season to begin, time to see if all their hard work had paid off.

"Let's meet in the foyer," instructed Martie. Krista knew it was because Noah was waiting for them right outside the door. All the girls gathered around him.

Martie smiled at the team. "I want you to go out there and do what we've practiced. Curtis's team might have the reputation, but this team has the heart, right? You find a person to mark and stay with them." The girls nodded. "Carla, you stay on number eleven," she instructed. "That's their best forward. Let's win the fifty-fifties. Forwards, be relentless. Keep taking shots. If you take a shot and miss, don't let down. Garbage goals are still goals."

Krista knew "garbage goals" were Charlie's specialty. Rather than requiring a lot of skill, those goals demanded quick thinking and tenacity. It was the same as the rebound in basketball—if someone took a shot on goal and it bounced off the post, Charlie was right there to knock it in and get the point.

Krista had watched Charlie work with Noah in practice on finishing every play. It grated on Krista that Charlie was clearly Noah's favorite. Charlie was never *anybody's* favorite.

pretty
TOUGH

Now Noah turned to Jamie. "Jamie—as captain, you'll lead the team in a warm-up, just like in practice." Krista looked on, wishing it were her.

"Okay, everyone," he said. "Hands in."

Everyone put their hands into the middle. As Krista put hers in, she noticed Charlie waiting until Carla put hers down, making for a barrier between them.

Krista frowned. Even on game day, Charlie couldn't get past whatever her stupid problem was.

Martie slapped her hand on top of the pile.

In unison, they all chanted, "Let's go, B-dub! Let's go, BANANAS!" in honor of the team's "favorite" healthy snack.

Krista pressed her lips together. It was time to play.

Charlie couldn't deny it. She was a nervous wreck. It was as if a butterfly colony had taken up residence in her internal organs. Her B-plus high was long gone, that thrill replaced with a stomach-twisting fear that she couldn't shake even as she ran with her teammates around the perimeter of the field.

She had been nervous since the moment she woke up this morning, which was at precisely 4:32 a.m. She tried to go back to sleep, but when she couldn't, she slipped out of bed and into her bathing suit, ripped sweatpants, and a hoodie, grabbed her neglected surfboard, and made the familiar trek down the beach. Martie would kill Charlie if she knew she was surfing the day of a game, but Charlie couldn't resist the waves.

It felt good to be back in the water and on her board, navigating the waves instead of around her sister. Her heart began pumping when she looked at the horizon and saw a killer set coming in. She caught wave after wave, cutting back and forth as she rode all the way to the beach. Paddling out again, the familiar burn started to penetrate her arms, but she noticed that she also cut through the water faster. A month of training had made her stronger than she'd even realized.

When she finally grabbed her surfboard and headed up onto the beach, she couldn't help noticing her old lifeguard station. She hadn't been there in ages. It almost looked lonely all by itself, so she took a few extra minutes to sit on the railing, stare at the water, and prepare for her first game in a long time.

Now, as the girls jogged around the perimeter of the field, Charlie tried to keep her gaze forward and her mind on what she was doing, but she couldn't help noticing the girls from Curtis. Something must be different in the water fountains down there because these girls were huge. Not fat, but scary, plow-you-down-and-not-even-feel-it huge. Charlie gulped as she watched them run the perimeter in two militaristic lines. While Erica and Buffi and some of the other girls were laughing and joking around, the Curtis girls were expressionless, focused . . . and gigantic!

Charlie took a spot next to Carla and Darcy for stretches. Darcy, as keeper, was eyeing the forwards nervously.

"Are your parents here?" Carla asked Charlie. Charlie glanced toward the bleachers. Both her parents were sitting there, and her father looked nervous. At least one of them always tried to make Krista's games. Now they were both here for Krista.

And, Charlie supposed, for her.

"There they are." Charlie pointed them out to Carla. Her mom waved over enthusiastically. Ugh! Embarrassing.

"Are yours here?" Carla asked Darcy.

Darcy looked around. "Not yet, but they will be. My parents have never missed a game in my whole life."

Charlie got the impression that wasn't a good thing. She looked up in the stands again and saw Pickle cheering wildly.

"Go, Charlie!" she yelled. "Go, Carla! Let's go, Darcy!"

Charlie smiled. Pickle: the ultimate good sport.

Darcy took her spot in the goal box as the girls rotated through shooting, passing, and heading drills. Charlie could hear Darcy's dad shouting instructions to Darcy from the stands. Each time he yelled, Darcy looked like she wanted to throw up. Charlie wished Darcy's dad would just zip it.

Krista interrupted Charlie's thoughts, calling the team into a huddle. Carla jogged over, and Krista put a hand on Carla's shoulder.

Charlie stared. Such a simple gesture, full of kindness and encouragement, so why couldn't she and Krista manage it with each other?

"Isn't Jamie the team captain?" Charlie asked, feigning ignorance as she joined the circle. "Shouldn't *she* be calling the huddle?"

Krista glared. Meanwhile, Charlie took stock of her teammates.

Ruthie shook out her hands and legs nervously.

Carla jumped around, barely able to stand still.

Heather took deep breaths as she grabbed onto her mass of curls and tightened her ponytail, securing it in place.

"Those defenders look really big," Ruthie worried.

"Yeah, well, their forwards aren't exactly munchkins either," Carla added. "Especially number eleven." They all simultaneously and non-subtly glanced over their shoulders, scanning the field for number eleven.

"Oooooh," Darcy groaned, scrunching up her face. Number eleven looked to be five feet, eight inches of pure muscle. The sleeves of her jersey had been tucked in like a tank top, revealing her bulging arms.

"I bet she could bench-press Ruthie," Julie thought out loud. Ruthie looked terrified.

Krista tried to refocus the team. "It doesn't matter if they're bigger, okay? We know what we can do."

"Run?" Heather joked.

pretty
TOUGH

"Exactly," Krista said. "We run fast and we run hard. We get to the ball first. Everybody focus on what we've practiced. We're probably not going to win the ball from these girls—"

Charlie interrupted. "You don't know that."

"Charlie!" Carla nudged her in the side.

"What?" Charlie knew she shouldn't have spoken, but who was Krista to say what the girls could and couldn't do? And why was Carla sticking up for her?

"I'm just saying," Charlie continued. "Who psyches up a team by telling them what they *can't* do . . . ?"

Krista took a deep breath.

"What I think she meant," Jamie, the team captain, explained, "is that we'd be better off as a team making clean, direct passes to each other. We don't want the ball in the air. Keep it on the ground so we can rely on our strengths—our speed and skill. Okay?"

"Okay," the B-dub players chorused.

The *Rocky* theme started pumping from the field's speakers—the traditional signal that the game was about to begin.

Jen put her hand in the center. "One more time, hands in." The girls did their cheer again, and Martie pulled Charlie aside.

"Charlie," she said sternly. "I don't ever want to hear you disrespect your sister like that again."

"What?" Charlie gasped. "But she's—"

"No buts," Martie interrupted. "You're not sitting around your kitchen table at home. When you're in that huddle or on the field, she's your teammate. If you don't like the way she's doing something, you save it for after the game or talk to me or Noah."

Charlie shrugged defensively. "Fine. I'm—I'm sorry."

Martie softened a little. "Don't be sorry. Just don't let it happen again. Now have a good game."

The whistle blew, signifying the end of warm-ups. Charlie jogged over to the bench with tears in her eyes. Any focus she had managed to attain was instantaneously gone. Now everything just looked blurry and confusing, except for her sister's perfect image, which was as clear as day.

From the moment the game started, Krista sensed trouble. It had begun back in the huddle when Charlie had the audacity to challenge her right there in front of everyone. She wished Charlie played for the other team so she could kick her right in the shin. At the very least, she hoped Charlie got turf toe.

As the starting lineup jogged to their positions, Krista kept her gaze down at the grass. She knew she could do this. She knew she could help lead the team to their first win, but Charlie's comment had hurt.

Charlie had no idea how bad it felt that she wasn't captain. She wanted to lead this team—and she had grown used to the spotlight. Not having it felt, well, awful.

Brooks had said it a thousand times—you simply had to look the part and people would buy it. Krista had imagined that if she looked like a beautiful, confident, self-assured person, she would be one.

What she didn't count on was that as put-together as she looked on the outside, on the inside she sometimes felt like a mess. The field had been the only place where her insecurities couldn't faze her. Now, thanks to Charlie, they had crept in here too.

You can do this, Krista thought, trying to stay in the zone. "We got this, B-dub," she shouted to her teammates. "Come on!"

The whistle blew. The first game of the season had begun.

For Charlie, the game was a combination of extremes. On the one hand, she produced—running tirelessly, trying to get open, trying to get a shot on goal. Her coaches were impressed by her energy and so, it seemed, was the crowd.

On the other hand—she had produced nothing.

Ruthless and aggressive, Charlie was actually more like the Curtis girls—less technically skilled and more apt to just plow someone down. So far, she'd been open enough to make three shots on goal.

So far, all of them had been deflected by the Curtis keeper.

Pickle, who was sitting with Benji and a few of the guys from the boys' JV team, went crazy in the stands every time Charlie took a shot. In fact, she could hear their voices yelling, "Char-lie, Char-lie, Char-lie," throughout the entire first half.

Amazing, Charlie thought. Was that cheering actually for her?

Noah encouraged from the sidelines. "Way to play, Charlie. Stay aggressive."

Charlie felt elated. Until she saw Krista get body-checked and lose the ball . . . again. Krista's chest hit the ground as the ball sailed down the field, heading danger-ously toward the goalkeeper, Darcy.

"Sweep back, sweep back!" Darcy yelled, barking orders from the goal box. Jamie moved between a Cur-tis forward and the goal box while in the midfield Krista stood up slowly. Too slowly.

How dramatic, Charlie thought.

Krista continued to shout instructions to the team, as if she had any right after losing the ball.

"You definitely deserve an Emmy," Charlie called out as she ran by. Then her voice filled with faux concern. "Or did you actually break a nail?"

"Get lost, Charlie," Krista spat back.

Charlie shook her head. Krista tried to talk tough, but in the end, she was about as hard as a bowl of Jell-O.

One minute before the first half ended, Curtis was up

pretty
TOUGH

one–zero. Martie shouted calmly but directly from the sidelines.

"One minute, B-dub," she yelled. "Be aggressive. You want this."

She stared hard at Charlie. "Listen to Krista!"

Charlie was taken aback but managed a nod. So far, she'd blocked out Krista's voice the same way she blocked out Regan's—ignoring her like an undeserved slight in the hallway or the garbage truck on Tuesday mornings.

Stopping a shot after a corner kick, Darcy threw the ball to Carla, who made a run out of backfield up the right side, shouting to Krista to switch with her. As Krista moved back onto defense, Carla passed the ball to Charlie, who knocked into one defender, turning to prevent her from getting her foot on the ball. The defender tugged at Charlie's jersey as Charlie struggled to control and hold on to the ball. With Krista moving back to defense, it was Carla barking instructions at her, trying to let her know what was happening on the field.

Charlie could feel her heart pounding out of her chest. She swore she could hear it, too. Everything around her was a blur; all she was focused on was the goal box. She knew in this moment all eyes were on her. This was her chance. It was as if she were moving in slow motion. Time seemed to slow down.

Charlie's foot connected with the ball as she kicked it hard and low to the ground. It shot past the Curtis keeper's outstretched right foot and hit the back of the net.

"Goooooooooal!" Noah yelled from the sidelines.

Charlie thrust her hands in the air, then spun around to face her teammates, who engulfed her in a huge hug. She saw Carla sprinting down the field toward her. She threw her arms around her.

"You did it!" Carla yelled. "You did it!"

"*We* did it," Charlie corrected, screaming over the roar of the home crowd.

In the stands, Charlie could see her parents cheering.

"Great job, Charlie," her dad yelled, cupping his hands around his mouth to be heard. Charlie gave a small wave and raced to join her team in the huddle.

Martie patted Charlie and Carla on their backs. "Way to communicate, you two."

Krista nodded and muttered, "Nice shot."

Charlie pretended she couldn't hear. It was too little, too late.

Krista took a swig from her Gatorade bottle as Martie psyched them up for the second half. "It's tied up, one–one. . . . It's still anybody's game."

Charlie was fired up. Beachwood definitely had a chance to win.

"Let's focus now for the second half," Martie said. "Carla and Jamie—nice communication between you two.

Strong on defense. Julie, keep your head in the game. No shots, no goals, right?"

Carla and the other defenders nodded.

But seven minutes later, there had been both a shot and a goal. Charlie watched the ball hit the back of Beachwood's net, Darcy's fingertips just skimming it, as the spinning ball flew past her.

"Shoot," Charlie muttered, kicking the ground. Curtis had scored on the rebound.

On the sidelines, Martie pulled Zaida off the bench. Zaida ran onto the field toward the Beachwood goal.

Darcy knew what that meant. She was out.

Darcy's shoulders sagged even as she tried to leave the field with her head held high. There was light applause from the stands. Darcy's dad could be heard above the others, booing the replacement of his daughter.

"It's not Darcy's fault," Charlie complained to Ruthie. "It's Curtis. The only reason they score is because they play dirty."

"It's true," Ruthie agreed. "Three of their players have been yellow carded already."

When Zaida was in place, Charlie took her spot in the middle of the field, waiting for the ref to blow the whistle. If these Curtis girls were going to try to lawn mow over everyone, she wasn't going to sit back and be the grass.

THUNK! Charlie started with the ball.

"Back to me," Krista yelled. "Back to me."

Charlie ignored her. She wasn't passing just so Krista could lose the ball for the zillionth time. Charlie passed to Jen and ran around the Curtis striker. Jen danced around the ball, using her patented fancy footwork to avoid losing it.

Clearly, before becoming a track star, Jen played soccer. She had finesse. The Curtis brutes were no match for her speed and agility.

Krista barked instructions to Jen. "Send it to Charlie," she yelled as she ran upfield. "Charlie, turn, turn."

Charlie ignored Krista. She ran straight toward the goal but was heavily marked by an opposing defender.

"Charlie, turn!" Krista insisted. She paused for a second, then changed her tune. "Me, me, me," she yelled. "Got me back."

Jen knocked the ball back to Krista, but Curtis intercepted, kicking the ball high.

The ball hovered right above Krista. It was the perfect time for a header.

"Mine!" Krista yelled. "Mine!" But Charlie could see her already backing away. She ran to get under it herself.

Charlie jumped to head the ball.

BAM! Charlie's skull collided first with the ball, then Krista's face. The ball flew out–of–bounds.

"Ow!" Krista yelled, grabbing her nose and doubling over. "What the hell is your problem?"

"You were in the way!" Charlie shrugged.

pretty **TOUGH**

"What about the letters *M-I-N-E* don't you understand?" Krista screeched. She removed her hand to be heard.

It was then that Charlie saw it—a tiny trickle of blood running from her sister's nose.

"Oh," Charlie said lamely. "That sucks."

Martie called Krista off the field. Karen ran on to take her place. Charlie watched as Noah jogged up to Krista and handed her a towel.

"Hey. You okay, Kris?" he asked, concerned.

Krista wiped away tears with the back of her hand and knelt on the ground.

"Coach!" Charlie yelled.

But Noah didn't respond. He knelt beside Krista, putting a hand on her shoulder. Charlie couldn't take her eyes off them.

So, is that it? she wondered. *A few tears from Krista and I'm invisible again?*

A Curtis player threw the ball in and Charlie snapped back into the action of the game. She jumped in front of the ball, intercepting it and trapping it between her feet. Turning her back to the Curtis player, she managed to pass the ball upfield to Ruthie, who was open. Charlie sprinted toward the eighteen box.

"Got your square," she yelled when she was parallel to Ruthie. Ruthie passed to Charlie.

Karen shouted instructions from behind. "Help back,

help back," she said, indicating that she was right behind her. Charlie knocked the ball back to Karen and suddenly, BAM! Charlie was facedown on the ground.

"What the hell?" Charlie groaned and looked up to see number eleven. She had flat-out pushed her!

Noah shouted from the sidelines in her defense. "Do you have eyes?" he screamed at the ref. "That was a foul!"

Charlie didn't like being pushed, but she was pleased Noah was back to paying attention to soccer.

"Shake it off, Charlie," Martie called to her. "Keep your head in it."

Charlie watched the B-dub defenders successfully navigate the ball out of their eighteen. Karen had the ball and was looking for someone to pass it to.

"Got me," Charlie yelled. "Turn right, got me!" Just as Charlie's foot connected with the ball, SLAM! She was bodychecked again. She hit the ground with a thud.

Number eleven tried to conceal a laugh as the whistle blew for a time-out.

Charlie popped up quickly, as if she were on her surfboard, and ran to the sidelines. "What is she *doing*?" she yelled to Noah before she reached him.

"They're just playing dirty," he said. He placed his hands on her shoulders and looked deep into her eyes. "Don't let 'em get away with it. Okay?"

Charlie felt her chin. It was bleeding. She wiped the blood away with the back of her hand.

Krista's eyes narrowed nearby. "Yeah, Charlie," she called softly. "Don't let them get away with playing *dirty.*"

Charlie's blood boiled at Krista's accusation. But just because her sister was too much of a pretty girl to dig in, Charlie didn't have to play that way too.

The whistle blew again, and Charlie took the ball near Curtis's goal box. Karen was right next to her, and Charlie tried to pass, but number eleven blocked her, slamming into her, tugging at her jersey, causing her to lose the ball as it got booted upfield by another Curtis defender.

That was it. Charlie was *not* going to be pushed down. Not on her field.

Between Regan and Krista, she'd had enough of that for one lifetime.

Charlie tipped her head down like a bull racing toward a bright red piece of fabric and plowed straight into number eleven's stomach. She tackled her to the ground, practically inside Curtis's goal box.

The crowd went wild.

The ref ran over, pulling Charlie off number eleven.

"What're you doing, you freak?" number eleven yelled.

Charlie wriggled away from the ref's grasp. "Let go of me. She started it."

The ref blew the whistle. Krista looked on in disbelief from the sidelines. Even Carla stared, horrified. The ref held up a red card and handed it to Charlie. She was thrown out of the game.

"No way! She pushed me first," Charlie protested. The ref blew his whistle again, and she had no choice but to take a place beside Krista on the bench.

The home crowd booed Charlie's benching, but to no avail.

As Charlie watched from the sidelines, Curtis went on to win the game, four–two.

Krista slammed her locker door shut and spun around, ready to wring her sister's neck. Some of the girls had played amazingly well. But in spite of that, they lost. And Krista blamed one person: Charlie.

When Charlie finally slunk into the locker room, Krista made a beeline for her, confronting her at the door.

"Nice game, Cujo," she snapped, referring to the old movie about a killer dog. "You're lucky my nose isn't broken."

"A movie reference—how clever," Charlie shot back. "Did Brooks help you come up with that when you were taken out of the game for being such a crybaby?"

"At least I wasn't kicked out for being a psychopath!" Krista countered.

Charlie pushed by her, heading toward her locker. Krista followed. "We lost that game because of *you!*"

Charlie spun around. "You're even more delusional than you look! You're the one who's supposed to know what you're doing out there. But you were getting creamed. Your strategy didn't make any sense!"

"What doesn't make sense about 'that ball's mine'?" Krista asked. Her voice was loud and shrill—and starting to quiver.

The room grew quiet. The other girls started to stare.

"Well, God forbid you don't get everything you want," Charlie spat. "God forbid you let me have the spotlight for once."

"News flash," replied Krista angrily. "This is about soccer, not whatever stupid thing you're teen angsting about this week. When we're on that field, your job is to listen."

"Listen? To someone too scared to go for the ball?" Charlie laughed. "I don't think so."

Krista's entire body shook. Then SLAP! Her hand made contact with Charlie's cheek.

Charlie's face burned red. Krista wasn't sure if it was from the force of the blow or from embarrassment. Charlie lunged for her, pushing her into a row of lockers, just as Martie burst in the door.

Martie grabbed Charlie and pulled her off Krista. "Stop it! Stop it right now," she shouted. "Or you're *both* off the team."

Charlie and Krista reluctantly stepped apart.

"Both of you—in my office." Martie seethed. "Now."

• • •

Thirty seconds later, Charlie and Krista sat in Martie's office, listening as she ranted about their horrible behavior on the field.

"What *was* that?" Martie asked Charlie. "Plowing into another player? She didn't even have the ball!"

Charlie tried to defend herself. "You saw all those times she knocked me down? Someone needed to show her that she couldn't get away with it."

"No." Martie shook her head. "If you get pulled out for sinking to her level—or in this case, lower—what good does it do us? You didn't use your judgment. You let the whole team down."

Charlie hung her head. Then Martie turned to Krista.

"And you—when is it okay to scream at another player, let alone your own sister? She's your teammate, Krista. You're supposed to be working *with* her, not in spite of her."

Krista's mouth dropped open. "How can you expect me to be a teammate to someone who doesn't even care?" she asked. "She didn't *want* to play soccer. She only joined this team to make my life miserable."

"Do you honestly think your sister doesn't care?" Martie asked in disbelief.

Krista folded her arms. "Charlie cares about one thing. Herself."

"Excuse me?" Charlie retorted. "A—I'm in the room, and B—the only reason I took that header is because everyone knows *you're scared of them!*"

pretty
TOUGH

Krista stopped short. She felt tears brimming around the corners of her eyes.

Did everyone know? Really?

She sat in her chair sullenly. Martie softened a little.

"Look, you're both amazing players," she said. "This team needs both of you. The way I see it, I have three choices. One, I can alternate putting you on the field, which means neither of you will play as much as you want to. Two, one of you can quit the team. Or . . ." She paused.

Krista looked up. "Or what?"

"Or three, you can learn to get along."

Krista looked at Charlie. It was doubtful.

"What you do off the field, that's your business," Martie continued. "If you guys want to make each other miserable, that's your choice. But tell me this: as much as you hate each other—and I realize you really do *hate* each other—don't you hate losing even more?"

Krista could see Charlie glance at her out of the corner of her eye.

"Yeah," Krista answered. "I want to win. Especially after I've worked so hard."

"We've *all* worked hard," Charlie spat. Martie interrupted before another brawl could erupt. "Then here's the deal. You both want to play on this team? You call a truce on the field."

"And if we can't?" Charlie mumbled.

"Try tennis."

With that, Martie gathered her things and left the room.

eight

As soon as Krista plunked down next to Brooks, she knew something was up. It was the Monday after the first game, and Brooks, Buffi, and Julie were on the lawn, huddled together reading something. As Krista took out her lunch, they quickly tried to put it away.

"What's going on?" Krista asked suspiciously. "What were you reading?"

"Nothing." Buffi shrugged.

"So . . . uh, you and Cam are going to homecoming together, right?" Julie jumped in.

"Yeah . . ." Krista said.

Homecoming, still three weeks away, wasn't exactly on her mind. Julie's attempt to change the subject was entirely too transparent.

"Seriously, what were you guys reading?" Krista asked.

The girls exchanged a look between them.

"Give it to her." Brooks sighed.

Buffi handed it over—the latest edition of Beachwood's newspaper, the *Sand Dollar*. Krista flipped Buffi's copy to the back. She came face-to-face with a half-page picture of herself and Charlie in Friday's game against Curtis.

In the picture, Charlie was getting slide tackled as Krista stood watching in the background. Krista scanned the article in disbelief:

B-DUB WOMEN PROVING THEY'RE PRETTY TOUGH

Thanks to the efforts of two sisters, Beachwood women's soccer might have finally found its place on the SoCal athletic map. And despite their loss to perennial rival Curtis, this team, coached by alumna Martie Reese, has a bright future, and the Brown sisters are among the stars that shine brightest.

Although senior Krista Brown is strategic head of this team, it's her younger sister, Charlie, who provides the emotion and heart. Krista plays communicatively but cautiously, whereas her younger sister takes every hit, bodycheck, and slide tackle. Their approach is best indicated in their appearance at the end of the game—for Krista, every hair is still in place, while Charlie would fit in better on the boys' squad. Caked in mud and even bleeding, Charlie Brown looks like she's been in battle.

"Krista is a smart, skilled, experienced athlete. Charlie is a fighter," commented Coach

Reese. "She's the one out there who doesn't care what people think—she just wants to get the job done."

This was evident Friday when Charlie was red carded for a violent run-in with an opposing team's player. Volunteer coach Noah Riley didn't condone the sophomore's actions but said, "She proved one thing. She's fearless and won't be beaten down. You can't teach that. Charlie plays like she has nothing to lose."

Other standouts include Jamie Bonter, the team captain, Carla Hernandez, and Julie Theiser, who together anchor the Wildcats' solid defense, and junior forward Jen Schwartzott. See the Wildcats' next home game next Tuesday.

"I can't believe this," Krista gasped, looking at her friends in shock.

"It's not that bad," Julie said comfortingly.

Krista stared at her. Had Julie sniffed too much rubber cement?

Buffi tried to change the subject. "So, Brooks—are you really taking Noah to homecoming?"

Brooks threw a grape at Buffi. It bounced off her forehead. "How many times do I have to tell you? My crush on Noah Riley is as over as purple UGG boots." She pointed toward Buffi's feet.

Buffi looked down. "These? But . . . I love my UGGs."

Krista crumpled up the article, not wanting to deal. "Missy, you can do about a thousand times better than Noah anyway. That guy sucks."

She didn't add that if Noah wasn't giving her the time of day—*as her coach*—then Brooks had about as much of a chance snagging him as she had snagging a role in an Oscar-worthy movie.

Brooks challenged her. "Really? Well, if Noah sucks so much, why do you get mad when he pays more attention to Charlie than you?"

Krista's jaw dropped at Brooks's not-so-veiled accusation. "What?"

"It's true," Buffi put in. "Every time Noah takes Charlie off to the side, it's like the air around you bursts into flames."

"I don't know what're you talking about!" Krista exclaimed. "I don't get mad. I—"

"Whatever." Brooks shrugged. "You think he's cute. I get it. Believe me. You don't have to be so defensive about it."

The bell rang. Lunch was over.

"*I'm not defensive,*" Krista pressed. "And may I remind you that I have a boyfriend? A boyfriend I *love*? I do not think Noah is cute."

She stared at her best friend, worried. Did Brooks really think she had a thing for Noah?

Brooks gathered her stuff to go to fifth period. "It's fine. Maybe you have a crush on him, maybe you don't. I mean, what do I care?"

"I don't know—you're the one who brought it up."

"Yeah," Brooks muttered. "Yeah, sorry I did *that*."

She took off, leaving Krista standing there, staring at the crumpled newspaper.

As the people around her droned on about the disgusting cafeteria food and the homecoming dance, Charlie chucked the school paper in the trash can and headed to geometry.

Caked in mud? Bleeding? One of the boys?

She wondered if Regan Holder had secretly penned the article. Last year, Regan had basically called her a lesbian in front of the entire cafeteria. Now she was being called a boy, in writing, for the entire school to witness. What guy was going to ask her out now?

"Charlie!" Carla called from down the hall. Charlie spun around as Carla and Pickle caught up with her.

"Guess what?" Pickle gushed. "Carla's got big news. *Huge!*"

Charlie looked at Carla expectantly. Maybe Krista had a zit the size of Texas on the tip of her nose. Or the article had just been a horrible dream.

"Nate—the goalie from JV—just asked me to homecoming!" Carla said breathlessly. "Can you believe it? Me!"

"And I'm going with Benji," Pickle said happily.

Benji? Nate? Charlie felt her heart sink down into her Skechers. First the article . . . now this. Was there a label lower than "loser"? Oh yeah: boy.

"That's great," Charlie remarked dryly.

"And guess who wants to ask you?" Pickle said excitedly, grabbing Charlie's arm. "Harvey!"

Charlie felt like she was going to be sick. "*Harvey* Harvey?" she asked in complete disbelief . . . and not the good kind. "Like, the roof jumper?"

"Yeah." Carla and Pickle nodded simultaneously.

Charlie couldn't even muster a response. Was that supposed to make her feel better? Instead, she turned the corner into the math wing, where she saw Regan and her friends huddled around the paper, laughing.

She ducked quickly into her geometry classroom, wondering how much more of this she could take. Would she spend her entire high school career being ugly and dateless and "violent"?

She hadn't been foolish enough to think she'd have a date, but when she daydreamed in class, she could imagine going to homecoming with Carla and Pickle. The three of them would stand against the wooden wall where the bleachers were housed and make fun of all the lame girls like Regan singing "Paradise by the Dashboard Light" at the top of their lungs.

Carla, Pickle, and Charlie would laugh, not caring that no

one had bothered to ask them to dance when the slow songs were played back to back to back—relentless, like death.

Now, instead, Carla would be dancing with Nate and Pickle would be dancing with Benji while Charlie sat at home alone, watching reruns on *Nick at Nite*. That pathetic thought made Charlie want to cry. She wiped tears away with the back of her hand. Good thing that stupid reporter couldn't see her now. He'd probably write a follow-up article. *Breaking news!* the headline would read. *Tough sister caught crying actual tears.*

Whatever. She didn't need to put on a fancy dress in order to feel popular—she wasn't popular anyway . . . and a dress wasn't going to change that.

Charlie decided to think about one thing and one thing only: soccer. She'd made a promise to Martie to form an on-field truce with Krista, and Charlie had to admit, it was even harder than she thought it would be.

Getting along with Krista was pure torture. The results, however, were undeniable. In the sixteen days since their nightmare game against Curtis, Beachwood had won every game but one, which they'd lost in overtime.

On the field, if not off it, Krista and Charlie made a pretty good team.

A week before homecoming, Charlie jogged down to the locker room to grab her uniform. Then she headed toward the bus to their away game at Lincoln. She passed Krista and Julie on the stairs.

"Hustle up, Charlie," Krista instructed. "You're going to miss the bus."

Charlie glared at her sister. She wanted to share some choice words with her. She wanted to tell her to stuff it. But there was that pesky truce. "Coming. I'm coming," Charlie muttered.

Two hours later and halfway through the game, Charlie was red-faced and dripping with sweat. She could pretty much guarantee that her hair was a wreck, not salon perfect like Krista's, but she was doing what she'd promised Martie: listening and responding.

If Krista said, "Move right," then Charlie went right.

If Krista said, "Cut back," then Charlie cut back.

Krista could have said, "Jump," and Charlie would have asked how high. And every time she heard her sister's annoying voice—how was it that even her *voice* sounded blond?—she wanted to scream, "SHUT UP!"

Still, as Charlie's foot connected with the ball, she had to admit it was going well. The ball sailed into the top-right corner of the goal for Charlie's third score of the day. B-dub was winning. Again!

For the third time, the Beachwood section of the crowd went wild. Charlie's teammates tackled her happily, knocking her onto the ground.

Carla couldn't believe it. "This is incredible!" she cheered. "Three goals in the first half!"

Carla and her defenders hadn't let a single goal in either. Julie and Erica could have been doing cartwheels or picking dandelions for all it mattered—neither one had put her foot on the ball the entire game.

Krista made her way over and extended a hand to help Charlie up. She smiled. "Great job," she gasped, out of breath.

Charlie looked at her sister and in that moment knew she had a choice. She could make an effort—or she could be her usual self.

Charlie smiled and took Krista's hand. "Thanks," she said, hopping up. "We did it together." Then she squinted, tilted her head, and made a face. "You have something right here," she said, indicating the base of her right nostril.

Krista gasped and touched her nose, horrified.

"I think it's been there a while," Charlie continued.

Krista shot a glance at Noah, then ran for a tissue.

Charlie chuckled. Things between her and Krista were going okay, but that didn't mean she couldn't have a *little* fun. She gave a wave to Pickle and Benji—two fans in the stands who were cheering like crazy.

"Go, Charlie," Pickle yelled.

"Good grief, Charlie Brown! Who wants some PEANUTS?" Benji asked. He held up a stereo "say anything" style and blasted the *Charlie Brown* theme song.

The fans in the stands went wild.

Charlie stopped, stunned. People cheering, music blasting—it was incredible. Was all this really for her?

Noah grabbed Charlie and put an arm around her. "That was awesome . . . but you should have gotten it in on the first shot, not the rebound."

Charlie gave him a look. "You're very demanding for someone who just stands on the sidelines screaming at people."

He squirted her with water from his water bottle, and she pushed him playfully. He stumbled back into Krista, accidentally stepping on her toes.

"Oh, sorry," Noah said. "I didn't see you there."

Krista looked at him, her eyes narrowed. Charlie stifled a laugh.

All of her goals, her friendship with Noah, the crowd going crazy—it had to be eating Krista up.

Finally, Charlie thought. *This is all mine, and Krista can't touch it.*

Krista and Cam were eating nachos . . . well, Cam was eating nachos. Krista munched a few chips and secretly longed to stuff her mouth full of gooey cheese and guacamole. In between nibbles, she filled Cam in on her last game.

"So . . . he squirts water on her, then she pushes

him . . ." Krista ranted. "I mean, what is that? Are they, like, BFFs now?"

Cam dipped his nachos in guacamole, then crammed the chip into his mouth. "I 'on' oh," he said, mouth full.

"And it's not just that. It's like I don't even exist on the field. You'd think the center mid would get a little attention, right? But no! Everyone's going crazy for Charlie! It's like people only care about the person who scores—as if the ball just magically gets to their feet inside the eighteen."

Cam wiped his face with a paper napkin. "Well, Krista, maybe it's just—"

"Oh, and this is great," she continued. "That guy who writes the stupid sports articles in the *Sand Dollar*? He interviewed Charlie after the game. Like, he wanted a quote or something. From *Charlie!*"

Cam looked confused. "Didn't she score like four or five goals by the end?"

"She scored four goals and assisted on one," she corrected him.

"Same difference." Cam shrugged.

"No, it is not!" Krista exploded. "*I'm* the only one at Beachwood who's scored five goals during a game. . . ."

"Okay, okay," Cam said, holding his hands up in surrender. "But Kris, what do you care if Charlie gets some play? She's the hot new thing, and you have to admit, she's good."

Krista stopped. Did Cam just say that her little sister was *hot?* Charlie, with her chipped black nail polish and clothes that would look better on a boy? The world really *was* coming to an end.

"Fine. She's good," Krista admitted. "I'm just better. I don't know why Noah's all wrapped up in—"

Cam frowned. "You know, Brooks told me you were bent out of shape about Noah not giving you the time of day."

Krista stared at her boyfriend, her mouth open in surprise. "What?"

Cam looked down at his plate and played with a slice of jalapeño. "Brooks says you're tweaking about the fact that Noah doesn't pay any attention to you. I don't need to, uh, worry about him. Do I?"

"Worry? No!" Krista yelped. "And that's—that's just not fair. I want Noah and Martie to notice me *as a player*. I can't believe Brooks would say that."

Cam said nothing for a few minutes. Then he tried changing the subject. "So I—I booked a hotel room for homecoming."

Krista almost choked on a chip. "What?"

They were over halfway through the season, and homecoming was now only a few days away.

"Game's on Friday." Cam shrugged. "Dance is on Saturday, and some of the guys on the team, the seniors—they all got rooms at the Vista on PCH."

"The Vista?" Krista asked.

Sometimes, when she wasn't sure how to respond, she simply repeated what other people said to her. It was a trait

Charlie found incredibly annoying and pointed out often.

"It's cool there," Cam said, trying to sound casual. "They have big king beds and hot tubs in the room that are heart-shaped."

"Heart-shaped?"

Cam seemed a little nervous. "Well, more triangle-shaped, but you know . . . kind of like a heart—with pointy edges."

Krista thought about repeating "pointy edges," but common sense stopped her. She was beginning to sound ridiculous.

Krista gulped. A room? In a hotel by the highway? "I'll have to check with my parents, I guess."

Cam laughed. "Your parents? You think they're going to let you stay in a hotel room with me . . . alone?"

Krista bit her lip nervously. Of course they wouldn't. That was the point.

"Tell your parents you're staying at Brooks's," Cam instructed. He put his hand over hers. "Come on. We've been waiting for this night forever. I told all the guys we'd be going. Don't you—don't you want to?"

Krista shook off her insecurities and plastered on a smile. "Of course I do. Why wouldn't I?"

She said it so firmly, she almost convinced herself.

nine

Charlie couldn't believe she was actually at the homecoming game, like every other normal kid, cheering for Beachwood.

Carla and Pickle had called to invite her, and since it sounded marginally better than sitting at home, searching Google for links between random words like *death* and *mouse pads* or *bras* and *egg rolls*, she decided to join in.

Now she and Pickle were making their way back from the concession stand—with hot dogs and sodas for the group. She had been in line so long, she had no idea who was even winning.

Charlie was focusing on not spilling her orange soda when she was stopped by a couple of guys. A couple of *cute* guys.

"Hey," the blond one said. "Nice game against Lincoln last week. You're Charlie, right?"

"Uh, yeah," Charlie answered shyly.

The brown-haired one smiled. "Hey. I thought Krista was the soccer star of the family. But you? You're awesome out there."

They recognized both guys as juniors, and members of the boys soccer team. Charlie could feel herself blushing. Were they actually talking to *her*?

"Thanks," she practically whispered.

"What'd you score? Like three times?" the blond asked.

"Four," Pickle corrected him. "And one assist."

"I'm Kevin," the blond said, then pointed to his friend, who gave a wave. "That's Bryan."

"This is Pickle," Charlie said, and Pickle smiled.

"Pickle? That's cute." Kevin laughed. "So are you guys going to the dance tomorrow night or what?"

Pickle nodded. "I'm going, but Charlie—"

"Charlie! Charlie Brown," a voice chirped.

Charlie turned to find Regan Holder, wearing her cheerleading uniform and holding her pompoms in one hand. The other hand held a foam B-dub sports bottle.

No, Charlie thought, staring down at her shoes. *Please. Not now.*

Regan took a long sip from the water bottle. Charlie wondered if there really was just water in there. She placed a hand on Kevin's shoulder. "What do you need to know about Charlie Brown?" she smiled. "Ask me. I can tell you everything."

"Don't you have somewhere to be?" Charlie asked.

Kevin's eyebrows knit together in confusion. "Uh, we were just asking if Charlie was going to the dance."

Regan snorted a response. "Yeah, right. Maybe. If she's going with *her*." She pointed to Pickle and laughed.

Pickle frowned at Charlie. "What is she talking about?" she whispered.

Charlie's hands balled into fists. All this time, Pickle, Carla, and the other new girls hadn't heard the rumors. Regan was ruining everything. What would her friends think of her now?

"You guys trying to recruit her for the *boys'* team?" Regan continued with Kevin and Bryan. "I bet she'd fit right in." With that, Regan spun on her heel and flounced back toward the cheerleaderson the sidelines.

Charlie gnawed on her lower lip. What now? There was no way Bryan and Kevin were going to stick around. And Pickle! What would she think now that she knew about the rumor?

There was an awkward silence. Then Pickle let out a long laugh. "That girl has more issues than People magazine."

Kevin and Bryan cracked up. Even Charlie laughed, relieved.

As everyone had a chuckle at Regan's expense. Charlie's mouth hung open in amazement. None of what Regan said had mattered. At all.

Bryan turned his bright blue gaze back on Charlie. "So, you never answered our question. Are you going to the dance?"

Charlie smiled shyly. "I, uh—I hadn't really decided."

"You should go," Bryan said. "It'll be fun. I'll be there . . ."

Charlie blushed. "Sure, yeah. Okay."

The guys walked off.

Pickle squealed, grabbed Charlie's arm, and pulled her toward the stands. Charlie tried not to drop the drinks she was holding as they ran to their seats.

"What happened?" Carla asked, seeing Pickle's frantic approach. "Is everything okay?"

"Better than okay. Two junior boys just talked to her," Pickle said slowly, as if it were the news of the century, "and asked if she was going to homecoming!"

All the girls squealed.

"Wait. Are you kidding?" Darcy yelled. "You just were asked to homecoming?"

Charlie deflated a little.

"Not exactly," Pickle jumped in, "but they knew who she was from the soccer team—they totally were at the game last week, cheering her on. They remembered her name and everything!"

Ruthie jumped up and down. "Two junior boys know your name!"

"All right, all right." Charlie put a hand on her shoulder. "Ruthie, less caffeine."

Ruthie smiled sheepishly. "Sorry."

"Wait a minute," Carla said. "Does this mean you're going to homecoming?"

"I don't have a date." Charlie sighed.

"Maybe not." Carla grinned. "But if you play your cards right, by the time the dance is over, you will!"

Wearing a dress felt about as foreign as a kilt or clogs. Still, here Charlie was, staring at her own reflection in a turquoise, knee-length BCBG dress that had shown up on her bed yesterday afternoon.

Her mom, excited that Charlie was exhibiting signs of normal teenage girl–dom, had gone shopping on her behalf. There was a dress, beaded sandals with a tiny delicate heel, a matching handbag, earrings, and a necklace.

Charlie swept her hair back into a low ponytail with the part on the right side.

She made the part a little farther from the center than usual—she'd seen that hairstyle in a magazine once for wearing ponytails on special occasions.

She thought of asking Krista to borrow some of her makeup, then figured that if she tried to put it on herself, she'd look like a clown. Better to stick to the free samples from her mom's Clinique purchases that lined the top drawer in their shared bathroom.

Charlie put on a little mascara and lip gloss and hoped she'd done it right. She placed her hand on the bathroom knob and realized she didn't want to leave. Brooks, Buffi, and Julie were busy getting ready in Krista's room. Charlie didn't want to have to deal with them until Carla and Pickle and their dates showed up.

As if on cue, the doorbell rang. They were here—Carla with Nate and Pickle with Benji. Charlie took a deep breath and hoped Krista and her clones were locked in her room, discussing whose butt looked biggest in her dress.

Charlie grabbed her matching purse from her bed and hurried downstairs, where she saw her parents usher Nate and Carla into the foyer. Charlie stood at the top of the stairs, nervous. Her mom looked up.

"Charlie, your friends are here," she said, stating the obvious.

"I see them," Charlie snapped, then wanted to kick herself. Couldn't she have *not* been a brat for two seconds?

"Hi, Charlie." Carla waved nervously. Nate was already holding her hand. "You look great."

So did Carla. She was wearing a calf-length white dress with an empire waist and tiny buttons down the back. Against her dark skin, the creamy white dress looked even more incredible.

"You too," Charlie answered.

Pickle and Benji walked in a second later. Benji's jaw dropped. "Wow. That's a step up from shin guards and soccer cleats . . . Pretty hot for a cartoon character, Charlie Brown."

Charlie smiled and walked gingerly down the stairs.

"You know Nate, right?" Carla asked. "From the boys' team? He's the starting goalie. . . ."

Charlie gave an awkward wave. "Hey." She nodded to Nate.

He smiled back. "Hi, Charlie."

When she reached the bottom of the stairs, Carla grabbed her and pulled her into a hug. "You really do look awesome," she whispered in her ear. "You are going to knock those senior boys off their feet!"

"You think?" Charlie asked, disbelieving.

"I know!" Carla winked.

Charlie stared at her feet but couldn't suppress a tiny smile. Whether she wowed the seniors or not, it felt good to have a friend like Carla, who made her feel like she could.

Charlie's mom grabbed the digital camera. "I just want to get a few pictures before you go!"

Charlie's eyes widened in horror. No one had mentioned pictures. "Mom . . ." she mumbled under her breath.

"Just one," Emily Brown promised. "Get together. Look like you like each other," she joked. Charlie shuffled next to her friends and forced a smile. The picture snapped.

"Okay, bye," Charlie said hurriedly, not wanting to create another opportunity for a Kodak moment.

She was almost to the door when she noticed her mother dabbing at her eyes with a Kleenex. "You're beautiful, sweetheart," she whispered. "Have fun at the dance."

Krista looked around nervously as she and Cam walked into the gym, holding hands. They'd arrived in a group with the other guys on the team and their dates. Julie was with her new boyfriend, Todd (a cornerback), and Buffi was with her boyfriend, Shawn, who played defensive tackle. Brooks had bragged she was going to bring Frankie Muniz, but, no surprise, he hadn't been able to make it. So Brooks was arriving confident and solo. Cam had politely offered to be both their dates in the limo.

Brooks had laughed. "You wish, loser." But now she grabbed his hand. "Can I steal him for a dance?" she asked Krista.

Krista was more than happy to let Brooks take him. She'd heard the guys talking when they thought no one else was listening. They were all teasing Cam, congratulating him for finally "doing the deed."

The words made Krista's skin crawl. Did the entire team really need to know about tonight?

She had lied to her parents, packed a bag for the hotel, and now was panic-stricken. She didn't know if she wanted her first time to be at the Vista . . . in a triangle-shaped hot tub. But how was she supposed to break it to Cam?

She headed for the punch, wondering whether some-one had spiked it. Alcohol would make this night go a lot smoother. Too bad she didn't drink.

As she ladled the punch into her red plastic cup, Noah approached.

"Hey," he said, holding out his own glass. "Free refills?"

Krista smiled and poured him some punch. It was amazing how different Noah looked off the field.

Brooks would never admit it—especially not tonight—but Noah was roughly three times hotter out of uniform. He was wearing a rock-star-worthy black velvet blazer with a crisp white shirt, dark distressed jeans, and black loafers—all of it clearly designer.

Not that it mattered to Krista, of course.

"You're not spiking this stuff, are you?" he asked.

Krista shook her head.

He took a sip. "Too bad."

Krista took a sip too. There was an awkward silence. She wondered, what could they possibly have to talk about? Noah so obviously favored Charlie—and Krista was, well, the anti-Charlie. Somehow, she'd have to break the ice.

"So. You came all the way back from Europe to be a high school soccer coach," she began. "Is it everything you dreamed it would be?"

Noah corrected her. "*Volunteer* soccer coach. I do this for fun, remember? Not profit."

Krista smiled. "Even better."

Noah looked around. "Yeah, I might take Barcelona or Belgium over Beachwood, but hey. These are the cards I was dealt. You don't plan on getting injured."

"No, you don't," Krista agreed.

"You also don't let it scare you," Noah added.

"Excuse me?" Krista asked. She narrowed her eyes.

"I know about your injury last year," Noah told her. "I'm just saying, if you're lucky enough to still be able to play, you have to stay aggressive. Going after a header's not going to rip open your knee."

"Hey," Krista snapped, defensive. "I go after plenty of things, okay?"

Noah shrugged. "Okay."

There was more silence between them. Krista bit her lip. She had something on her mind. She just had to get up the guts to say it. She took a deep breath.

"So should I be honored?" she asked. "That you're finally giving me the time of day?"

"What's that supposed to mean?" Noah asked.

Krista shrugged, trying to be playful. "You and Martie . . . I don't know. . . . I know I'm not Charlie, so . . ." She trailed off. She couldn't bring herself to actually say it—to admit that her coaches clearly liked Charlie better than her. She quickly backed out of the conversation she started.

"Never mind. I don't know what I'm saying," she said, holding up her cup. "It must be all the punch."

Noah smiled. "Yeah, it must be."

They stared at all the kids dancing. Krista noticed Cam still on the dance floor with Brooks, who was gyrating like a Vegas belly dancer.

"There is a reason I give more attention to Charlie than you," Noah said finally. "Two reasons, actually." He looked around, as if he was letting her in on a secret he didn't want anyone else to hear.

"One," he explained. "Charlie is a great player and a great kid—and it seems like she could use a little . . . support."

Krista recoiled at the accusation. Was Noah implying that she hadn't supported Charlie? Well, she'd tried, but she refused to deal with Charlie's petty insults and childish putdowns.

"And two," he continued, "sometimes the person you want to talk to the most is the one you end up talking to the least."

Krista felt confused. "That makes absolutely no sense."

"I'm your coach," Noah said slowly. "Volunteer or not, I'm your coach. There are certain rules."

Krista frowned. "Rules that keep you from acknowledging my existence? Or even talking to me?"

"Yes. If I'd like there to be more than that," he said.

Krista shook her head, still not understanding. "More than *what*?"

Then it slowly dawned on her. Was Noah trying to say

what she thought he was saying? Was Noah interested in her?

Her eyes darted around as she wondered if anyone had noticed their conversation. When her gaze landed on Brooks and Cam, she saw that they were staring right at her.

"I—I have to go," she told Noah. She quickly plastered on a smile and ran out to the dance floor.

Charlie had been dreading it from the minute they walked into the dance. As the first chords of an old Aerosmith tune blared over the speakers, she felt her heart sink.

There it was—the inevitable slow song.

Up until now, Charlie had been having a good time— maybe even a great one. She'd danced most of the night in a big circle with Carla, Nate, Benji, and Pickle. She had even paired off with the guys whenever their dates got tired.

But now what? Charlie wondered, standing alone on the gym's hardwood floor.

Most everyone had coupled up.

Carla and Nate were already close together, swaying to the music. Benji was in the process of teaching Pickle some insane dance moves. Pickle couldn't stop laughing long enough to try them.

Charlie glanced around. No question, *her* best move was a quick escape to the ladies' room. She turned around to make a hasty retreat and nearly ran into a boy standing behind her.

"Hey. Where's the fire?" he asked.

Charlie blinked. It was Bryan. She hardly recognized him in his black suit and tie. He looked amazing.

"Uh—hi," she stammered. "You were—I was just—" She pointed toward the nearest exit.

"I was hoping I'd see you here." Bryan smiled, his eyes warm. "You look great."

"Thanks," she managed, fidgeting with the clasp on her evening bag.

Bryan nodded. There was a moment of awkward silence.

"So—slow song," he observed. He held out his hand. "Want to dance?"

Charlie stared. She'd never done this before. Did she have a choice? Maybe she could just say no. Maybe she could—

"Come on. Don't look so scared," Bryan said, a little laugh in his voice. "Though maybe you should be. There's a good chance I'll step on your feet."

Charlie chuckled. Her palms felt cold and sweaty at the same time. "I—um—"

She wanted to say she didn't dance. She wanted to say that the only physical contact she'd ever had with a boy was when she collided with one during dodgeball. But before she could muster a suitable response, Bryan grabbed her hand and pulled her out to the dance floor.

Charlie forced a smile. She glanced over at Carla and caught her eye. When Carla saw what was happening, she broke into a huge grin and gave Charlie a quick, covert thumbs-up.

Charlie grimaced her response, and Carla laughed. Then Bryan turned to face her. Ignoring the butterflies in her stomach, Charlie rested her hands on Bryan's shoulders and allowed him to place his hands on her waist.

"So," he began. "I heard you surf—"

As they swayed to the music, Bryan asked Charlie questions—about surfing and soccer, about her family and hobbies. Charlie was impressed. It was as if he actually cared.

The Aerosmith song ended, and Charlie stepped away from Bryan. "So, thanks. That was nice."

"Wait," he said, hanging on to her hand. "They usually play the slow ones back-to-back. Want to try again?"

Charlie sighed. "Listen, this is nice and all, but you don't have to."

"I don't have to what?" Bryan asked.

"This," Charlie clarified. "Dance with me."

Bryan shook his head. "Why wouldn't I want to dance with you?"

Charlie's eyes darted toward Regan, holding court with three sophomore guys across the gym.

"You don't have to feel sorry for me," she said. "I'm

pretty
TOUGH

not one of the popular girls, I'm here alone, and I'm cool with it, really."

Bryan turned and **noticed** Regan himself. He smiled. "Charlie, do you really think I care what other people say about you?"

Charlie gulped. "But you must have heard about . . . the rumors?"

Bryan shrugged. "So? They're just stupid rumors. All I know is, I saw you yesterday, we talked, and I've been looking forward to seeing you again ever since."

"Really?" Charlie asked.

"Yeah," Bryan answered. "I've seen you play. You're tough, you're smart, and as far as I'm concerned, you're the most interesting person here."

Charlie felt a lump form in her throat. "I am?"

Bryan nodded. "I like talking to you, Charlie. But to be honest, there *is* another reason I asked you to dance."

Oh no. Here it comes, Charlie thought. She swallowed hard.

Bryan leaned in to whisper, "I'm hoping you'll give me a few pointers on my game. I start a club league in the spring."

Charlie studied Bryan's eyes. They were calm, steady.

He took her hand. "Hey. Instead of worrying about what everyone else thinks, why don't you just enjoy yourself? After all, it's just a dance."

As Bryan slid his arms around Charlie's waist, she

glanced around the gym. She felt like a spotlight was on them, like everyone was staring. But when she really focused, she saw that everyone was engrossed in their own slow dances, too busy gazing into the eyes of their boy-friends or girlfriends to pay any attention to her.

For once, she fit in perfectly.

When the dance was over, Charlie asked her friends to wait up while she made a trip to the ladies' room.

Bryan had offered to drive her home, and truthfully, she was tempted, but she'd come with Carla, Pickle, and the boys, and it was only right to leave with them.

Besides, Bryan had taken her phone number—and promised he'd see her in school on Monday. The mere thought made Charlie's dread about walking Beachwood's halls fade away.

She was leaving a ladies' room stall when she found Krista standing in front of the mirror, touching up her already-perfect makeup.

"Hey," she said as she washed her hands.

"Hey," Krista managed as she powdered her nose. Her tone was cool, disinterested.

Charlie glanced at her sister, reflected in the dingy bathroom mirror. She thought for a second, taking her time with the soap and water.

Since Martie's enforced truce, things had been a little bit better between them. And everything else had gone well tonight—surprisingly so. Maybe she could try with Krista. Maybe, if she could just get her talking . . .

"So, uh, you're going out after this?" Charlie asked.

"Mmm-hmm," Krista answered.

Charlie smiled. "I'm going with Carla and Pickle to get some ice cream, I think."

"That's nice," Krista stated. There was a long silence as she reapplied her lipstick.

"Mom and Dad said you're sleeping over at Brooks's?" Charlie asked.

Krista shot her a suspicious glance, one perfect eyebrow arched. "That's right."

"Well, I hope you guys have fun," Charlie told her. "Whatever you're up to."

Krista's eyes narrowed. She snapped her evening bag shut. "What do you mean, *whatever you're up to?*"

"Nothing." Charlie shrugged. "You just, you didn't say where you were going and—"

Krista took a step toward her. "Have you been eavesdropping on my phone conversations again?"

"Wh-what?" Charlie sputtered. "No! I just—"

"You know what, Charlie? I don't know what you're trying to imply, but what I do is none of your business. Just stay out of my space, and I'll stay out of yours. Okay?" Krista turned and clicked out of the bathroom on her high heels.

The door swung shut. Charlie dried her hands, a heaviness settling on her heart.

Yes, tonight had gone wonderfully, unbelievably well. Perhaps she shouldn't have pressed her luck.

When Cam pulled his Blazer into the parking lot of the Vista, Krista's heart began racing. She was really doing this. She was really going to spend the night with Cam.

She waited in the car as he checked in, nervously texting with Brooks on her Sidekick:

KRISTA: I JUST DON'T KNOW IF I SHOULD DO IT.
BROOKS: Hello? Caps lock. Stop yelling. And you have to do it. He put rose petals on the bed.
KRISTA: How do you know?
BROOKS: He needed some ideas. So I helped him.

Krista stared at the message in surprise. She was *so* happy that the prospective loss of her virginity had brought Brooks and Cam together. She typed:
KRISTA: You and Cam were here together?
BROOKS: Missy, relax. It was all for you. And it's not like we've never been in a hotel room together before.

There it was. That not-so-subtle reminder that Brooks had been here first. It made Krista's stomach turn.

Cam tapped on the window and, smiling, held up the key to the room.

pretty
TOUGH

Krista gulped. It was now or never.

She walked into the suite and thought it *was* beauti-ful—at least as beautiful as a room at the Vista with a triangle-shaped hot tub could be. Rose petals were scattered all over the bed. There were candles on the night-stands and the dresser. Cam had gone to a lot of trouble to make the place look nice.

Krista was overwhelmed by a mixture of pleasure and dread. The expression on her face must have been something less than Cam was expecting.

"What's wrong?" he asked. "Don't you like it?"

Krista nodded, a smile plastered on her face. "Of course I do," she said quickly. "It's perfect. Very romantic."

Cam walked over to the triangle tub and pressed a button. There was a rumble of jets and the water began to bubble. The tub looked warm and inviting, but Krista stood staring at it, perfectly still.

"Should we try it out?" Cam asked, slipping off his shoes. "The water's warm."

Krista smiled. "Yeah, sure. Let's do it."

Quickly, she caught herself.

"I—I don't mean 'do it,'" she stammered. "I mean, do what you just suggested. Go into the Jacuzzi. That sounds—nice."

Cam walked over to her and placed his hands on her shoulders. "What's wrong?" he asked again.

Thoughts swirled in Krista's head.

"Nothing," she told him.

Cam took her hands in his, leaned down, and softly kissed her.

His lips were warm, gentle. Then gradually, more insistent. Krista returned the kiss, trying to lose herself in the feeling, but images flashed in her mind.

Cam's friends high fiving him as he left the dance. Gazing at her with a knowing look in their eyes.

Brooks's text message. *It's not like we've never been in a hotel room together before.*

And Noah, for some reason.

"Kris," Cam whispered her name. His hands moved to the zipper on her dress.

Krista felt every muscle in her body tense. But why? she wondered. Wasn't she being ridiculous? Plenty of girls her age had done it . . . and Cam was the right guy for her. He was. She wanted to go to college with him and marry him and spend the rest of her life with him . . . didn't she?

Cam began to unzip her dress. Krista squeezed her eyes shut.

She tried to focus, to calm the doubts inside her, but her mind came to rest on just one thought: she wasn't ready to have sex.

It wasn't Cam or the Vista. Or the fact that she'd lied to her parents about where she was. It was *everything*. But all of that was so difficult to say.

Somehow, she had to make Cam understand.

"Wait," she whispered.

Cam either didn't hear or pretended not to.

"Wait," she said more forcefully, putting a hand against his chest.

Cam stopped, frowned. "What is it?"

"I—I'm sorry," Krista began. "I'm just—I'm not sure."

Cam tried to pull her close. "Aw, Kris, you're just nervous. It's all right. Everything is perfect. Just stop thinking about it."

He began to kiss her again, but she pulled away. "Cam, I just—please, can we talk about it for a minute?"

Cam threw his hands in the air. "Are you kidding? What the hell is there to talk about?" He sat down on the bed, dejected.

"The petals," Krista whispered. "You're crushing them."

Cam pushed the petals off the bed. "I don't care about them," he said, his voice rising. "Krista, you said we could do this. Don't you—don't you love me?"

"I do." She felt tears spilling out of her eyes. "I just—I don't feel right about it."

"You don't feel right? What about my feelings?" Cam asked. "I've waited for you, Krista . . . and you know I've had other offers."

Krista recoiled. What was he trying to say?

"I'm sorry." She choked out the words. "I thought I was ready, but—"

"But what?" Cam asked. "It's always something with you. Always some trauma."

He paused, shook his head. "Brooks said you would pull something like this."

Krista gasped. She felt her throat tighten, like someone was gripping it and squeezing. "Brooks?"

"She said you'd make this about you," he muttered, raking his fingers through his hair. "God. Do you have any idea what the guys are going to say?"

Krista didn't care about the guys on the team. She knew Cam didn't either—not really. She had to make him see her side of it.

She wiped her cheeks with the back of her hand. "Cam, please. I know you're upset. I just—maybe I need a little more time."

Cam stared at her, his eyes hard. "Is that what this is really about?"

She frowned, confused. "Of course. What else would it be?"

He folded his arms across his chest. "I saw you talking to Noah tonight."

Krista blinked. "What does Noah Riley have to do with anything?"

"You tell me," he said.

There was a moment of silence, but inside, Krista's

mind raced, a million thoughts screaming in her brain. It sounded like a riot.

"It's not Noah," she insisted, getting her bearings at last. "It's not anything like that. Can't—can't I just not want to? Can't that be good enough for you?"

Cam regarded her coolly. "You know what, Kris? It's not. Get your stuff. I'm taking you home."

"What?" Krista gasped. "I didn't say we had to leave. The night doesn't have to be over."

Cam grabbed the key off the nightstand. "It is, all right? It's over."

She gaped at him.

"You were always just a substitute anyway," he added in an undertone.

Krista closed her eyes. She hoped to God Cam wasn't saying what it sounded like he was saying.

"What?" she whispered.

"C'mon." Cam laughed bitterly. "You knew that, didn't you? Deep down? It was always Brooks."

Charlie was lying in bed, her mind replaying her dance with Bryan, when she heard a car pull into the driveway. She got up and made her way over to the window.

It was dark out, but in the moonlight, she could see clearly enough. It was Cam's car dropping Krista off.

Wasn't Krista supposed to be at Brooks's?

Charlie knew that was a likely story, but if Brooks was

Krista's cover with Cam, what on earth was she doing home in the middle of the night?

Charlie watched Krista get out of the car slowly. She lingered at the open passenger's side door, talking. Then, as she was speaking, Cam's hand shot out from the driver's side and pulled it shut.

Krista stood there, silent in her homecoming dress, her high-heeled shoes dangling from her hand.

Cam revved the engine and peeled out. Krista gazed after his taillights, and as they blinked out of sight, she crumpled to the ground.

Charlie watched, frozen. She could see Krista's whole body shaking. Her beautiful green dress formed a satin puddle around her feet.

Charlie felt a squeezing in her chest. Sure, she gave Krista a hard time on the field, calling her a baby, but she never saw her sister shed a tear, let alone sob. It just wasn't like her.

Charlie knew Krista was hurt. She wasn't sure what to do, but she was surprised to discover that she couldn't just stand there. She had to do something.

She moved away from her window and flipped on her light. She shoved her feet into her slippers and grabbed a sweatshirt off the floor. Making her way downstairs, she sneaked quietly, not wanting to wake her parents. She sidestepped the squeaky floorboard at the bottom of the stairs and opened the front door.

pretty
TOUGH

It was the end of October, and already the air felt crisp and cool. It was misty out, and Charlie instantly felt the moisture on her face. She made her way over to her sister.

"Krista," she called softly, standing above her. "Are you okay?"

Krista didn't respond. It was like she didn't even hear Charlie. Or know she was there.

"Krista?" Charlie said again, looking to make sure it *was* her sister and not some random girl from homecoming, too drunk to find her house. "Do you want to come inside? It's kind of . . . starting to rain."

Krista didn't budge. She began sobbing even harder, Charlie thought, to the point where she was almost choking.

The squeezing in Charlie's heart grew stronger. She looked around helplessly. Then slowly, she knelt beside Krista and put her arms around her.

Still sobbing, Krista let her body fall into Charlie's. To her surprise, Charlie felt tears pricking the corners of her own eyes. She still didn't know what was wrong, but she said the only thing she could think of.

"Everything's going to be okay," Charlie whispered. "It will be."

ten

When Krista woke up the morning after home-coming, it seemed that everything in her life had been turned upside down—some things for the better, others for the worse.

She remembered Cam leaving her outside last night on her parents' lawn, and she remembered somebody hugging her, comforting her. What she couldn't believe was that it had been Charlie there in the driveway, holding her close.

Charlie sat with her while she cried for God knows how long.

Charlie took her inside and made her some toast with peanut butter.

And Charlie finally put her to bed when the birds outside had started to chirp.

Krista groggily looked at her clock. It was only 8 a.m. She thought about everything that had happened last night—the hotel, Cam, what he'd said about Brooks—and her stomach turned.

It's always been Brooks, he'd said.

Krista gave a bitter chuckle. She had spent the better part of the soccer season worrying about being in Charlie's shadow. Now she realized she had spent her entire relationship with Cam in Brooks's—and she hadn't even known it.

Today, she wasn't the soccer team's star. She wasn't half of the most-celebrated couple in school, and, quite possibly, her enormous popularity would suffer for it.

But how much did it all matter? Surely, she was something without all that . . . wasn't she?

Krista got up and grabbed a sweatshirt, making her way to her sister's bedroom. She pushed open the door and looked inside. Charlie's bed was empty.

She walked into the kitchen. Her dad was there, reading the Sunday paper. He looked up from the finance section as she passed.

"I thought you were staying at Brooks's last night," he said as he sipped his coffee.

"Yeah," Krista lied. "I was tired, so . . . Do you know where Charlie is?"

"Surfing. At least that's what I'm assuming since she's gone and her board is too."

"Thanks." Krista nodded and slipped on her flip-flops by the door. She grabbed her keys off the counter. "Be right back."

When she pulled up at the beach a few minutes later, she could see her sister among a few other surfers. Charlie was clearly the youngest of the bunch . . . and the best. Krista climbed down the rocks, careful not to slip, and took a seat in the sand.

She watched her sister paddling, spinning, and catching wave after wave. She couldn't help being impressed. Although Charlie had learned to surf a few years ago on a family vacation in Hawaii, she'd gotten serious about it last year—serious enough to compete and win in local competitions. Krista knew that when school had become rough for Charlie—when Regan ditched her—surfing became her outlet.

Krista watched Charlie bobbing up and down, just a speck out there in the surf, and felt her sadness deepen. She knew how much Regan had meant to Charlie—they'd been best friends since they were little. Then it all just—fell apart.

Krista had been in the cafeteria that day last year, but at the time, she didn't think much of it.

She remembered looking over, seeing Charlie yelling, causing a scene.

So what? she thought at the time. Charlie had always been a bit temperamental, and Krista didn't want her sister's tantrum tainting her image—so she sat there watching the whole thing unfold.

Later that day, the rumors began.

"Did you hear your sister attacked some girl at lunch?" Harvey Harvey had asked her. "Guess she wanted a bite of her fish sticks."

"What?" Krista asked. She didn't have time for Harvey Harvey and his creepy weirdness.

"I guess she was jealous of this girl and her boyfriend." Harvey shrugged.

"Jealous?" Krista repeated. Her confusion must have been obvious because Harvey quickly clarified.

"I didn't know your sister played for *the other team*." He leaned in with a lecherous expression. "Does it run in the family? 'Cause that's hot."

Krista shuddered and walked away from Harvey, unwilling to dignify his question with an answer. But for the rest of the day, she was bombarded with news of the rumor about Charlie.

She could have taken Charlie's side—could have defended her. But that seemed like inviting trouble.

So instead, she had laughed it off, saying she had no idea what her sister's deal was . . . but no, it definitely did *not* run in the family.

After that, Charlie became hostile. Whenever Krista spoke, she was quick with a cut down or snide remark. She withdrew into her own world, and a permanent distance opened up between them.

Now, as Krista thought about it, she had a realization. By not having the courage to stick up for Charlie, she'd somehow validated what Regan had said. By not having Charlie's back, *she'd* perpetuated the rumor. By blowing it off and making a joke of it, *she'd* driven a wedge between them.

It should have been different. She should have supported Charlie—no matter what.

Krista shook her head. Charlie's anger . . . maybe it was *her* fault.

She scanned the vast horizon and noticed another huge set rolling in. The swells were gigantic, and she could see that Charlie was going to go for it.

Krista watched as Charlie paddled hard to catch the first wave. She popped up on the fall line and floated across the top of the wave. A moment later, she dropped back down into the face.

Krista watched, amazed. Charlie was unbelievable. She had absolutely no fear.

Charlie accelerated down the face of the wave. The nose of her surfboard pearled underwater. Krista gasped as Charlie pitched out. Her surfboard flipped behind her and she toppled end over end over end, finally disappearing into the froth.

Krista sat up, expecting to see Charlie pop up out of the water. But after a few seconds . . . nothing.

Krista jumped up and ran for the beach. Still Charlie was nowhere to be seen.

"Charlie!" she called. No answer.

Krista kicked off her shoes and dove into the water. Where was her sister? She looked around frantically. A wave crashed over her, knocking her back. When she resurfaced, she pushed her hair out of her face and rubbed the water out of her eyes.

"Krista?" a voice asked, surprised.

There was Charlie bobbing right next to her, one hand on her surfboard. "What're you doing?"

"You didn't—come—up." Krista gasped for breath. "I thought something had happened."

"So you dove in?" Charlie looked completely shocked.

"I couldn't exactly let you die," Krista said. Feeling awkward, she turned it into a joke. "Not unless I killed you myself."

Charlie smirked. Krista put a hand on Charlie's surfboard. She didn't know what to say as they bobbed up and down in the ocean. Every second of silence felt like an hour.

"Well, thanks," Charlie offered.

"Yeah," Krista said. "You too."

"Don't mention it." Charlie kicked through the water, and together the girls let the tide carry them toward the beach.

Later that night, Krista drove over to Brooks's house. She needed to talk—about everything. Cam's hurtful words weren't Brooks's fault, she reasoned. Brooks couldn't help it if every guy in school wanted to date her.

And sure, Brooks had told Cam some thoughtless things, but that was just her way. She was truthful to the point of bluntness. And she was still Krista's best friend . . . probably the only person in the world who could understand this mess.

Thank God Brooks's parents were away for the weekend. Krista knew she'd really be able to let loose once she told Brooks the whole story.

Krista pulled into the Sheridans' driveway and stopped short. A black Blazer was parked in the driveway.

Cam's car, she realized with a jolt.

Krista's heart raced. What was *he* doing here?

She got a sick feeling in the pit of her stomach. She had to warn Brooks about what Cam had said last night—before he tried something stupid. She grabbed her cell phone and dialed Brooks's number.

As it rang, Krista spied a light in Brooks's bedroom window. She saw Brooks walk toward the window, fishing her phone out of her purse.

"Missy!" Brooks answered cheerfully. "What's up?"

Krista watched Brooks in the window. "I need to talk to you," she said. "Did you hear about me and Cam?"

"Yeah, I heard," Brooks said. "Don't worry, Missy—you can do *so* much better than that loser."

Through the window, Krista saw Brooks duck as a pillow was launched in her direction. She laughed.

Krista's eyes narrowed.

pretty
TOUGH

Wait a minute. Cam was in Brooks's house. Was he upstairs with her? *In her bedroom?*

She felt her face grow hot, turning red with anger. . . .

Then she stopped. Maybe she was overreacting.

"Um, what're you laughing at?" she asked.

"Oh, nothing," Brooks said. "I'm just watching TV."

"Really?" Krista asked. "So you're there alone?"

"Nobody here but us starlets," Brooks answered breezily.

Krista's jaw clenched, her fury building. Why would Brooks lie about being alone in her house? Why wouldn't she want Krista to know that Cam was there? There was only one reason. . . .

"So I was thinking of coming over," Krista continued, struggling to keep her voice calm. "I could really use a friend right now."

"Oooh, sorry," Brooks said. "I don't think I can. I have this big audition tomorrow. Tons of lines to memorize."

As Brooks spoke, Cam came up behind her and grabbed her around the waist. He kissed her neck.

Krista tasted something bitter in the back of her throat. She wanted to throw up on them both.

"Oh, really?" Krista responded, faux curiously. "Is it a different kind of role for you?"

"What d'ya mean?" Brooks asked. She turned to face Cam, playing with the buttons on his shirt.

"You know. Is it something different," Krista asked,

"or are you playing a two-faced liar who steals her best friend's boyfriend and doesn't even have the decency to let her friend know about it?"

"What?" Brooks pushed Cam off her. "What are you talking about, Missy?"

"Look out your window." Krista started the car and threw it into drive.

Brooks glanced down at the driveway and saw Krista's car. Krista saw a look of horror form on her face.

"Missy!" she called. "No, wait!"

"I don't think so," Krista said as she pulled into the street. "But I really hope you get that part, Brooks. You're just perfect for it."

She pressed the accelerator and peeled off.

Now that her truce with Krista had extended beyond the playing field, Charlie felt a huge weight off her shoulders. It wasn't as if one night had turned them into best friends, but at least she and Krista were no longer bitter enemies.

And now that Krista was no longer talking to Brooks, she seemed just a little more patient, a little less judgmental.

It made a huge difference during games. Everyone noticed—their teammates, Noah, Martie. . . .

With the tension between her and Krista gone, they could all just focus on soccer—and not a moment too soon. Today was their final game of the regular season. If they won, they'd beat out Westlake for a spot in the tournament, and their season would continue.

If not, the team would be packing it in till next fall, and the seniors would be packing it in forever.

Charlie ran her heart out, jumping in place to stay warm when the ball was down at the other end of the field. She had so much nervous energy it was hard to keep it all contained.

Downfield, Erica fought off a Ridgefield forward and switched field, passing a long ball to Heather on the opposite side. Heather stopped the ball with her chest and trapped it between her feet as she was attacked. She quickly passed to Krista, who ran with the ball, shouting directions to the forwards, surveying the field for a hole in the Ridgefield defense.

"Charlie, turn outside," Krista yelled, sending the ball upfield to her. Charlie spun around, the ball perfectly placed by her feet. She dribbled around a Ridgefield defender and turned again, shooting the ball unexpectedly from the outside, slipping to the ground as she did. It flew past their goalie and hit the bottom-left corner of the net. The Beachwood players on the bench cheered from the sidelines as the players on the field rushed Charlie. The crowd went wild. The *Peanuts* theme blared over the PA system. Charlie gave a low five to Krista.

"Nice pass," Charlie said, out of breath.

"Let's do it again," Krista said as Jamie clapped and continued to psych up the team. Noah gathered them over to him.

"Last home game, you guys," he said excitedly. "Let's put this one away." He grabbed Charlie around the shoulders. "Nice shot. I told you. You're a star." Charlie smiled. For the first time, she really felt like one.

Suddenly, in a totally un-Charlie-like display, she put her arms around his waist, giving him a hug.

"Whoa," he said. "What's this?" He gave her a pat on the back.

"Just thanks," Charlie said. "For everything."

He spun her around. "Got a few more minutes. Let's put another one in the net." She smiled and ran back out onto the field.

Within five minutes, Charlie had scored again. Beachwood went on to beat Ridgefield four–zero.

When the game ended, the entire Beachwood team rushed the field, including Martie and Noah.

"You did it, you guys!" Martie yelled.

The entire team huddled into a big circle. Some of the seniors were crying, happy that they were going to the championships in their last year.

Carla had a huge smile on her face. Her uniform was covered in dirt. She wrapped Charlie in a hug. "We did it!" she yelled. "I can't believe we did it!"

Jamie bent down to wipe blood from her knee.

Charlie just looked around, shocked. They all looked like they'd been in battle. Like Martie said, they really were warriors.

"What does this mean?" Ruthie asked. "Does this mean . . ." She was so excited, she didn't want to say it.

Martie smiled. "It means pack your bags. You'll be spending next weekend in Pomona. And if all goes well, we'll be state champions!" The girls' voices exploded into cheers. Charlie glanced up into the bleachers and saw Bryan cheering for her. A couple of sections away, her father and mother were waving their Beachwood pennants. She was about to wave back when Noah picked her up and spun her around.

Charlie felt dizzy from all the excitement, but she couldn't stop smiling. They really had done something incredible. And it wasn't over yet. Post-season had just begun.

With Noah in her corner, her friends at her side, and her sister on the same page, Charlie knew she'd be unbeatable.

After all the congratulations and the hoopla had died down, Krista made her way to the locker room to get her stuff. It had been an early game since today was Saturday. The sun was still out, and the sky was clear. She was excited for the rest of the day . . .

Except that she had no plans and nothing to be particularly excited about.

Martie came down to the locker room as Krista packed up her bag. She had a bunch of clothes stuffed in her locker that she *absolutely* needed to take home to wash.

"Nice playing today." Martie smiled. "Not that you need me to tell you that."

Krista couldn't help but smile.

"What?" Martie asked.

"Just—thanks," Krista said.

"For what?" Martie asked.

"It's just, you know, I've been waiting for you to say that all season," Krista tried to explain.

"Ah." Martie nodded. "Strategy."

"Huh?" Krista frowned, confused.

"When you started, all you wanted was my approval—validation from me that I knew you were the best player on this team. Remember hell week? That first day? That race with Charlie?"

Krista blushed, remembering how badly she'd behaved.

"Well, that day, I decided I wasn't going to give it to you. My approval, I mean. Because Krista, who cares what I think? Or what Noah thinks? Or what that ex-boyfriend of yours (who you're way too good for, by the way) thinks? I wanted you to learn that what matters is what *you* think. If you think you're the best player out there, every time you step onto that field, then you will be." Martie paused. "And for the record, I think you are."

Krista's face broke into a wide smile.

"So it's not about *getting* every header, it's about *going for* every one. And it's not so that I can tell you that you did a good job out there. It's so *you* know that you did your best. What matters isn't what everyone else thinks. It's what you know. I learned that a long time ago. And I know Charlie isn't the easiest kid to be a big sister to . . . but you keep trying. Think back to hell week. Hard work pays off." Martie smiled. "Now go enjoy your Saturday."

Krista floated out of the locker room and up the stairs. Despite everything else that had happened in the past two weeks, she felt amazing, like she could do anything.

As she headed to her car, she spotted Noah getting into his. She thought about what he told her at homecoming. Even then, there was chemistry between them. She decided to act fast before she lost her nerve.

"Hey, Noah!" she called. "Wait up!"

Noah turned, gave her a dazzling, dimpled grin. "Hey, Krista. Nice game today."

She jogged up to his car. "Thanks. Um, I was just wondering—I don't have any plans, and it's a beautiful day. Do you think you'd want to go grab a bite to eat?"

Noah squinted against the sun. "Actually, I'm meeting some of the varsity guys at the beach. For a pickup game."

"Oh." Krista was disappointed. That wasn't the answer she hoped to hear.

She considered for a minute. "Do you think they'd let a girl play?"

Noah blinked, surprised. "You just played an entire game. . . . Do you really want to play another one?"

"I'm younger than you," she teased, half embarrassed by her own boldness. "I have a lot more energy."

Noah laughed. "Right." He clicked his doors unlocked. "Get in. I'll drive."

Happily, Krista hopped in his car. She decided not to think too hard about making the first move. Maybe hanging out with Noah would lead somewhere; maybe it wouldn't.

Either way, she thought, *if Brooks Sheridan knew where I was sitting right now, she'd eat her own heart out.*

Fifteen minutes later, they arrived at the beach, where a pickup game was just starting up. The B-dub boys were in tournament contention too, and many of the guys tried to squeeze in as much practice and conditioning as they possibly could. The boys' program had always been phenomenal, which made it all the more frustrating when the girls' soccer program was poised to take a nosedive.

Now, Krista knew, the girls had a chance to be on top again—to prove they were just as good as the boys' team.

When Krista climbed out of Noah's car, she was surprised to see Carla down on the beach, playing with Nate as the two chased each other around in the sand. He grabbed her, threatening to throw her in the water, while she loudly protested. Krista smiled, watching. She had seen them at homecoming together but hadn't realized they were actually a couple.

As Krista approached, Nate set Carla down. She looked up. "Hey, is Charlie here?"

Krista shook her head. "She got a ride home with my parents after the game. Are you playing in the pickup game?"

Carla shrugged. "I don't know. They want me to, but I'm exhausted."

"Me too." Krista smiled. "I just didn't really want to sit at home."

"We could sit and cheer them on," Carla suggested.

Krista considered. "I'd kind of rather kick their butts."

Carla laughed. "Cool. Let's do it."

Noah divided up the teams, putting himself, Krista, Carla, and Nate on one team. The other team was made up of four guys. Krista took her usual place as center mid; Noah became the lone forward.

Playing on the beach, four on four, was fun and low pressure as they batted the ball around in the surf and sand. Noah shouted instructions to Krista, telling her to hustle for the ball, challenging her to play more aggressively. It was harder to move in the sand but less scary to dive and fall. It was a good training ground for the way she wanted to play on the grass.

Halfway through the game, an opposing offender jammed Carla up with the ball. Desperate to get the ball to Krista, Carla kicked wildly. The ball arced through the air—it was a header.

"Go for it, Kris!" Noah shouted. "Don't back down."

Krista couldn't disappoint him. She watched the ball sail toward her. She positioned herself beneath it, jumped up, and—BAM!—sent the ball screaming toward the goal.

On her way down, she collided with Jim from the other team and collapsed in the sand.

"Goal!" she heard Carla cheer.

Krista turned her head. Sure enough, she'd sent the ball past the other team's keeper. Her jaw dropped. She'd done it!

When she didn't move immediately, Noah ran over. "Krista!" He knelt next to her. "Oh, wow. Are you okay?"

Krista grabbed a handful of sand and threw it at Noah playfully. "I don't believe it!" She laughed, excited. "Did you see that? I did it!"

Noah's expression turned from worry to relief.

"Yeah." He smiled. "You did." He extended a strong hand. "Now up you go."

Krista grabbed hold, and Noah yanked her to her feet—a little too forcefully. She bumped into his chest and grabbed his arms to steady herself.

They stood there, still, just that way.

Krista was so close to Noah that she could smell his

sunblock. Her face was just inches from his. She peered up into Noah's eyes and could feel her whole body blushing.

A million thoughts ran through her brain. Mainly, that she and Noah were only two years apart—if he was still in high school, they would have probably been great friends . . . or maybe something more.

"Hey! Are you guys playing or having a staring contest?" Nate called.

Noah ticked his gaze downfield but didn't move an inch. "Easy there, sophomore. I just want to make sure my player's okay."

His eyes returned to Krista, searching. "Are you? Okay with this?"

Krista nodded, mute. She couldn't deny that she felt something between them. Not anymore.

"Good." Noah grinned and broke away from her.

"All set, you guys!" he called to the other players. "But look out—I think Krista's ready for some serious action."

Krista was starving by the time she, Noah, Nate, and Carla got a table at Mulberry Pizza. She was having the best time with everyone. She realized suddenly that she hadn't thought about Cam for hours, except for now, when she was thinking about how she hadn't thought about him . . . which really shouldn't count, right?

She and Carla laughed as they looked over the menu, wanting to order every single thing on it.

It was funny, Krista thought. Carla and Charlie were so close that she hadn't had a chance to know Carla outside soccer. Now, she discovered, Carla was funny, smart, and really sweet. Charlie was lucky to have found such a good friend.

"Okay, some other things I can't stand." Krista laughed, sipping on her Diet Coke. "Dave Matthews, *The Simpsons*, and the word *nipple*."

Carla burst out laughing. "Me too, me too," she agreed. "Especially *The Simpsons*."

"What? Who could possibly hate that show?" Noah asked. "It's un-American."

"I was born in Mexico," Carla pointed out.

"Well, you're excused," Noah conceded, "but Krista? You're on the hook for this one."

"I'm more concerned with *nipple*," Nate pointed out. "Who hates nipples?"

"Ew! Stop saying that word," Carla yelled. She and Krista burst out laughing again.

Nate threw his hands in the air playfully. "You're the one who brought it up!"

"It's not just that," Krista explained. "Any double-lettered word. *Bubble . . . puddle . . . ripple . . .*" She shivered. "Ew."

Noah shook his head. "You're a nut. A very cute nut, but a nut."

"I just know what I like." Krista smiled, catching

Noah's eye. He smiled back. She quickly looked away, embarrassed. Had that been too much?

Carla got up to go to the bathroom, and Krista made an excuse and followed. Girls always went to the bathroom in pairs, and it seemed like a good opportunity to put some space between her and Noah—just for a minute.

Hanging out with him was much too easy . . . and comfortable . . . and fun.

"So you and Nate are like *dating*, dating, huh?" Krista asked as she reapplied her lip gloss at the mirror. Carla emerged from the stall.

"Yeah, I guess we are." She smiled. "I really like him. I even met his mom last weekend."

"Whoa, meeting the parents. That's serious." Krista rubbed her lips together. "What does your mom think of him?"

A look of guilt crossed Carla's face as she turned on the water and clicked the soap dispenser twice.

Krista gasped. "She doesn't know?" she guessed.

Carla focused on washing her hands, as if it took every ounce of her attention.

"Why not?"

Carla shut of the water and grabbed a paper towel. "Because she'd never approve," she explained. "She'd call Nate a gringo and say that this is exactly why she didn't want me to go to this school. She'd probably yank me out before finals. I'm not allowed to even kiss boys, but Anglo boys? She'd probably put me in a convent.

"It's like, I know what I'm doing is wrong according to what my mom says," Carla continued. "But it doesn't feel wrong to me, you know? So if it doesn't feel wrong— is it wrong?"

Krista understood completely. She realized that after spending the day with Noah, she knew what it was like to want to be with someone who had been declared off-limits. How could she have wasted so much time caring about Cam when Noah had been right there all along?

"I wish I knew the answer," Krista lamented. "All I know is we have two really cute boys waiting for us out there . . ."

"And eating all our pizza." Carla laughed.

And together the girls walked out of the bathroom and went back to join their guys, who had in fact already eaten the large pizza between them.

"You have to!" Krista begged as they drove down Main Street.

"I'm stuffed. I couldn't possibly eat any more food," Noah complained.

Krista frowned at him playfully. "That's because you ate the entire pizza! I'm still starving!"

He laughed and reluctantly pulled into Coldstone Creamery, Krista's favorite ice-cream shop. There you could make your own flavors by adding any toppings you wanted, and they'd mix it for you right on the spot. Instead of small, medium, and large, the sizes were "like it," "love it," and "gotta have it."

Krista ordered a "gotta have it" and marveled at how good it felt not to have Brooks whispering in her ear, scolding her about calories.

Noah groaned. "What are you? A bottomless pit?"

"Maybe," she said. She sat down with her huge waffle bowl and scooped a tremendous spoonful into her mouth. *Mmmm.* It was so creamy and chocolaty and—

OW!!! Krista felt a piercing pain between her eyes. She grabbed her head in horror.

"Oh my God, ouch!" she yelped.

Noah laughed. "Brain freeze?"

"Not funny," Krista cried, being overly dramatic. "It hurts, I tell you! The pain!"

"You forced me in here, and now you want sympathy?" Noah chided.

She nodded violently, loving every minute. She could never be silly with Cam. With Noah, it just felt natural.

"Put your tongue on the roof of your mouth."

"Huh?" Krista asked.

"Put your tongue—flat—on the roof of your mouth. And rub it around. To warm it up."

Krista obeyed, and like that, her headache disappeared.

"Wow." She smiled. "Impressive. Got any more tongue tricks?"

She scooped another huge bite into her mouth.

Noah regarded her skeptically. "Are you sure you want to—"

"OW!" She grasped her head again.

"—do that?" he finished. As she writhed around in pain, he grabbed her waffle bowl of ice cream. "I'll keep that safe for you," he said as he scooped a giant bite into his own mouth.

It was just past eleven as Charlie tossed and turned in her bed. She couldn't sleep. Maybe it was the excitement of the game today, of knowing how hard she'd worked, of feeling that finally things were coming together . . . but she was wired. She wanted to call Carla or even Bryan, but it was way too late for phone calls.

Bryan—Charlie wondered if things were going well with him. He did call her now and then, and a couple of times he'd sat with her at lunch and walked her to class. But did that mean anything? Did he like her? Or did he *like her*, like her? It was hard to know.

She supposed she could ask Krista, but Charlie wasn't sure the two of them had been on good terms long enough for that.

Maybe she should run it past Noah at next practice. . . .

Yeah, that was an idea. He could give her a guy's opinion. And the two of them were certainly close.

Charlie popped out of bed, tired of being restless, and

slipped on her shoes. She hadn't been to her lifeguard station in a while. And for some reason, something was pulling her there tonight.

As she hopped on her bike and made her way down to the beach, she thought of how many nights she'd sat out there wishing her life could be different. And now it was.

She no longer felt like a misfit or an outcast. As she walked down the halls with Pickle and Carla, stopping to talk to Jamie and Zaida or Ruthie and Darcy, she finally felt like she belonged. Just yesterday, when she was eating lunch in the quad, Nate and a few other guys from the boys' team came and joined her. Carla wasn't even there yet. They sat with Charlie just because they wanted to.

Charlie thought back to the beginning of the season. To how she got into this whole soccer thing solely to spite her sister.

She couldn't believe how lucky she'd been. She didn't know if she deserved something so good after she'd started it for such bad reasons—to make her sister's life miserable.

She took the last turn toward the beach, the cold air blowing on her face. It felt so good to be outside. It was quiet this late. Everything seemed so still.

She couldn't help but smile as she thought of the game today. She didn't know what possessed her to hug Noah like that, right on the sidelines, with everyone watching. It occurred to her afterward that maybe it wasn't appropriate. Girl players couldn't just go around hugging their male coaches. But she just felt so much toward him.

Not in a boyfriend way—not at all.

It was all the encouragement he gave her, the pep talks, even the criticism—she knew they had a special bond. He made her feel like she was worth something, like she was somebody worth seeing.

It was rare that someone saw that when Krista was around to overshadow her—being more beautiful, more outgoing, more perfect. But Noah treated her like something special on the field, and because of that, she had become something special on the field.

She was no longer in her sister's shadow. That's what the hug had been for. It seemed like just saying "thank you" wasn't enough.

She rode her bike down the sandy path and stopped when the sand became too deep to pedal through. Hopping off her bike, she let it fall to the ground as she made her way toward her lifeguard station. It looked so lonely under the moonlight. Since it was already November, she knew no lifeguard had been there since the summer.

As she approached, she saw something strange. She wasn't sure, but it looked like two people were leaning against the railing, kissing. Charlie sighed. Never had anyone else been at her lifeguard station, and now the one

night she wanted to sit under the stars, two horny teen-
agers had designated it their make-out spot. Well, Charlie
wasn't going to put up with that. She'd come all the way
down here. She was going to enjoy it.

"Excuse me?" she called out, moving closer. The people didn't stop. She decided to be a little more forceful.

"HEY!" she yelled. "Do you mind? There are other
people here!"

Caught, the two people moved into the moonlight.

Charlie stopped short. She couldn't believe what she
was seeing. It was Noah and Krista. They were the ones
kissing. . . .

Charlie turned and sprinted for her bike.

"Charlie, wait!"

"Stop!"

She could hear them calling after her, but she didn't
stop until she reached her house.

eleven

The bell rang, signifying not only the end of classes, but the beginning of Thanksgiving break. Charlie grabbed her stuff from her locker and made her way out to the parking lot. There, the entire soccer team was waiting to pile into a motor coach headed for Pomona, California.

Charlie stood waiting with her bag, proud to be one of the lightest packers on the entire team. She shoved her backpack in the baggage area under the bus and climbed on. As she had been doing all week, she marched past Noah without saying a word. She headed for the back, where Carla was already seated.

The entire bus was buzzing with excitement. Charlie could feel the energy in the air. *This* was what they had trained for all season long, and now it was happening. They were driving out to Pomona for the state championships—a four-day elimination tournament played at night, under the lights.

There was just one problem—Charlie felt completely deflated. Seeing Noah and Krista together had drained every ounce of excitement out of her. Right now, soccer was the furthest thing from her mind. And Carla had noticed.

"Okay, that's it," Carla said, exasperated. "You've been moping around for the last few days. It's not like you, Charlie. You have to tell me. What. Is. Wrong?"

This was the seventh time Carla asked Charlie what was wrong in a forty-eight-hour period. She supposed she couldn't deny it anymore.

Charlie looked around. Everyone else was distracted, trying to figure out where they were going to sit and next to whom. Plus, a sheet of paper was circulating listing everyone's room assignments at the hotel.

Krista read the page and appeared to be freaking. Maybe she'd been separated from Buffi and Julie. Ha!

Carla leaned in close so she could hear Charlie's whispering.

"Okay, so last Saturday night," Charlie began explaining, "I couldn't sleep, so I went down to this lifeguard station that I hang out at, and when I got there, I saw Krista and Noah—"

"Wait," Carla interrupted. "You hang out at a lifeguard station?"

Charlie looked at Carla in disbelief. "That is *so* not the point! The point is, I saw Krista and Noah there—making out!"

She looked at Carla for a reaction. Horror, disgust, surprise—any one of those would have done the trick.

Instead, Carla had a sheepish grin on her face.

"What?" Charlie asked. "Why aren't you freaked?"

"Well, I hung out with them that day after the game, and—"

"Wait—you what?" Charlie interrupted.

Had she just heard that correctly? Carla had "hung out" with Krista . . . ? What was that about?

"There was a pickup game down at the beach," Carla explained. "Nate came to the game, then wanted to play. . . ."

"You played a pickup game *after* our game?"

"I didn't really want to, but Nate did, and I wanted to hang out with him before I went home. At first, I thought I'd just watch, but then, right before we started, Krista and Noah showed up. . . ."

Charlie pressed her lips together, trying to contain her emotions. "Okay. And then what?"

Carla hesitated. "Then we grabbed pizza afterward. All of us."

"*All* of us?" Charlie asked, in a tone that demanded an answer.

"I mean . . . me and Nate, Krista and Noah," Carla explained.

Charlie's mouth hung open. She couldn't believe this!

Carla paused. "What?" she asked. "Are you mad? It's not like you and Krista are fighting anymore."

"That doesn't mean we're *best friends*," Charlie snapped.

"Hey, I'm not best friends with her either. But Noah

and Nate used to be on the boys' team together and—"
Carla stopped short. "You know what? I don't have to jus-
tify this to you. We played soccer. We had pizza. So what?"

"*So what?*" Charlie snapped. This was unbelievable.
Didn't Carla get what was going on here?

"Come on, Charlie," Carla pleaded. "This is stupid. I
can be friends with you *and* Krista. . . ."

Charlie grabbed her stuff. "No, you can't. And it looks
like you made your choice."

She shoved past Carla and looked for a new seat.

The ride to Pomona was excruciating for Krista.
Mostly because she had to sit clear across the bus from
Noah and act like nothing had ever happened between
them.

Now she understood why it was easier to just ignore
each other. Once the dam was broken, there was nothing
you could do to stop the flood of emotion.

She hadn't meant for anything to happen between
them physically. But then, she was the one who'd suggested they head down to the beach, wasn't she?

She just hadn't been ready for the night to end. Being
with Noah was easy and fun. He liked her with absolutely
no physical expectations because it couldn't . . . or at least
wasn't supposed to . . . happen.

Which made it all the more surprising when Krista
leaned over and kissed him.

He'd pulled away instantly. "Krista . . . we can't."

Krista remembered looking down, embarrassed.

"Not that I don't want to," he quickly explained. "I mean, this is why I keep my distance. Ever since that day we went swimming during hell week—"

"You mean, when you peed in the water?" Krista reminded him, punching him playfully on the arm.

Noah defended his actions. "I was flirting!"

"Oh, what was next? Pulling my hair?" She laughed. "What're you, eight?"

Noah shrugged. "Maybe nine."

She smiled and stood up. He followed. "Wait—you're leaving?"

"I think I have to," she told him. "Because if I don't . . . I'm going to have to do this." She leaned in and kissed him again. This time, he didn't pull away.

It was a perfect kiss. Noah was sweet and tender. Krista never wanted it to end—

Then Charlie walked up and spotted them.

And now she was giving both of them the cold shoulder. Every time Krista tried to speak with her, Charlie just blew her off.

A honk of a car driving by jarred Krista from all her thoughts. They were turning in to the Marriott in Pomona, where the team would be staying for the next four days . . . assuming they made it to the end of the tournament.

As she gathered her stuff to go in and change for their practice session, she shared a secret smile with Noah. They'd made a pact that they didn't want to do anything to jeopardize the status of the team—and even though he was a volunteer coach, Krista guessed making out with a player, even one who was eighteen, wasn't encouraged.

Besides, they had plenty of time to be together *after* the soccer season was over . . . and now there were only four days left. Krista was determined to make the most of it.

Martie pulled Charlie aside after practice to ask what was wrong.

"You weren't listening to Krista, Carla, *or* Noah out there," she said. "What's up?"

"Nothing." Charlie shrugged. It had just been a stupid scrimmage. Who really cared if it went well?

Martie placed a hand on Charlie's shoulder. "Charlie, if you want to talk, I'm here. If not, do us all a favor and work it out. You've come too far to get red carded again. You're too good for that. Don't let your temper get the best of you."

Charlie pulled away. "Fine," she agreed.

When she said it, she had every intention of not flying off the handle. But just walking past Noah and Krista made her blood boil.

And to make matters worse, she was assigned a room

with Carla *and* Krista. The universe clearly had it in for her.

That night, Charlie sat on her bed with her iPod blasting in order to tune out Krista and Carla. She felt bad that she was tuning out Jamie in the process—but whatever. Jamie was a casualty in her new war of silence. As she sat, she flipped through a copy of *Teen People* that she'd borrowed from Jamie. Not because she had any intention of reading it, but because she had nothing else she could use to distract herself.

As her eyes pretended to scan a page on the dangers of eating disorders, she wondered if it was obvious she wasn't reading. Krista, Jamie, and Carla seemed too engrossed in a *Laguna Beach* marathon to notice that Charlie was sitting there, seething.

The longer she sat there, the more her intense dislike for her sister festered and grew. Just when Charlie was happy about her life—just when she had something that was hers and hers alone—Krista had come along and deliberately ruined it.

She had been dumped by Cam and Brooks, so what did she do? She turned around and stole Charlie's friends—friends she cherished—on a whim.

The more she thought of Krista and Noah together at *her* lifeguard station, the more her hatred became like the blister on her foot—a wound that hadn't healed all season long because every time it seemed to be getting better, the skin peeled back, exposing a raw, tender layer.

She felt completely alone. And the timing couldn't have been worse. She gave up pretending to read and crawled under the covers to try to get some sleep before the first game tomorrow.

Krista came up from the locker room and peered over at the Beachwood bleachers. They were absolutely packed. Pretty good, considering that Pomona was about a two-hour drive and it was Thanksgiving weekend. The boys' team had made the two-hour trek out to Pomona together and now lined the bottom row. Krista and Charlie's parents had made the drive as well. Krista noticed them looking for a place in the bleachers. Her dad gave her an encouraging fist pump, and she gave a small, polite wave. He'd stuffed a card into her suitcase yesterday that said, *A big shot is a little shot that keeps shooting.* When she'd read it this morning, she'd smiled. She'd wondered if he'd given one to Charlie, too.

Krista was stretching her calves when she felt something tap her on the head. Once. Then twice.

Krista looked up—it was the first few drops of rain.

Umbrellas opened in the stands as Beachwood began their first warm-up lap around the field.

By the second time around, the rain started to increase. Krista's heart raced. She hated playing in wet conditions and rarely did since it rained so infrequently in Southern California.

If she played tentatively when the sun was shining, slippery turf only exacerbated her problem. Cutting back quickly and slipping on the wet grass was like an invitation to retear her ligament. She tried not to think about it as the team rotated through their drills and stretches.

What she thought about instead was finding a way to force Charlie to talk to her—to work things out before the game started. If they wanted to win and move on in the tournament, they were going to need to work together. They couldn't blow it now.

As the defenders booted long balls back and forth, warming up their legs for goal kicks, the B-dub offense rotated through shooting drills that Darcy deflected. Krista lined up behind Charlie and tried to make peace with her.

"Charlie," Krista said, trying to keep her voice low. "I know you're avoiding me, but I really need to talk to you."

Charlie didn't even turn around. "Go to hell."

"What?"

Surely, she had misheard what Charlie just said.

"You heard me," Charlie snapped.

Ooo-kay. So she hadn't misheard.

"What is your problem?" Krista demanded. Here she was, trying to be nice, to reach out . . .

"To start? You." Charlie shot the ball past Darcy. Krista

took her turn and missed. She circled around and took her place behind Charlie again.

Time for another tactic. Maybe she could bait her sister into opening up. "You know what? Forget it. I don't what to know what's wrong. You have more issues than *Us Weekly*."

Charlie forced a laugh. "Great line. Which one of Brooks's bad movies did you get that one from? *Bitch on Wheels*?"

Despite her best intentions, Krista flared at the mention of Brooks's name. "She has nothing to do with this!" she snapped.

Charlie smiled. "What, sore subject? Now, what exactly happened—did you make out with Noah because Brooks is with Cam now? Or is she with Cam now because you decided to hook up with Noah?"

Krista gasped at the low blow. "Keep your voice down," she whispered.

"Why? To protect you? Look out for you? Have your back?" Charlie acted like these were novel concepts.

"Seriously, why are you being like this? You're acting like a jealous—"

Suddenly, a horrible idea dawned on Krista. "Oh my God. Do *you* have feelings for Noah? Is that what this is all about? You're jealous because he chose me over you. . . ."

"I do *not* like Noah," Charlie snapped. "Don't be insane." She paused. "Oops—too late."

The ref blew the whistle signifying the end of warm-ups. Krista watched Charlie jog to the sidelines.

She stared after her sister, dumbfounded. Was she lying about her feelings for Noah? It seemed unlikely. Krista had never gotten that vibe from her before.

So, then, what was her problem? Was she simply a psycho? Was it a miracle she hadn't popped out of the womb with horns and a pitchfork?

The rain came down even harder, soaking through Krista's uniform.

She bent down and retied her laces, as she always did when she was nervous. Then she did a quick last huddle with her teammates and coaches and took her place on the field.

Noah shouted at her, "Kris!"

She spun around and stared at him, surprised he was talking to her.

"Aggressive, okay? Go after this!"

She nodded, but her confidence was shaky.

As soon as the game started, Krista knew they were in serious, serious trouble. Not because of the downpour, but because she and Charlie were having a full-out break-down.

It started with simple commands that Charlie wasn't paying attention to—she wasn't even looking to find Ruthie and Jen. If she had the ball, she simply plowed forward on her own, as if she were the only player on the field. Even Noah was shouting to her from the sidelines. But apparently, Charlie wasn't listening. She was doing what Charlie did best when her defenses were up. She was pushing everyone away.

Now, in the middle of the second half, Beachwood finally had a chance to score. Krista, who was heavily guarding Madison's number four, saw a breakaway opportunity. She dribbled the ball upfield, telling Charlie to move back.

"Switch back," she yelled as she carried the ball forward, searching for a shot or a teammate to pass to.

But Charlie didn't move back. Instead, she charged at Krista. She was actually trying to steal the ball!

"What're you doing?" Krista yelled. "Get back! Get on four." The ball rebounded off Krista's leg, and number four from the opposing team trapped it. She broke away, heading to Beachwood's goal. Krista and Charlie frantically ran back to defend against Madison's offense. But the Beachwood team was so frazzled by Charlie's behavior that nobody was where they should have been. Carla and Erica had rushed up when Charlie and Krista started their tussle. Now there was just Julie and Jamie left to stop the opposing team. Outnumbering Beachwood, they easily scored.

Martie, normally calm, threw up her hands on the sidelines.

"What was that?" she screamed over the roar of Madison's fans.

Krista stared at the ground, angry, knowing exactly what it was: an amateurish mistake that might have cost them the game.

"Ever heard of moving back?" she yelled to Charlie. "What's wrong with you?"

"Ever heard of knowing your place?" Charlie spat the words. "You have your position. You don't have to try to steal mine."

Krista couldn't believe this. Were they talking about soccer now—or Noah?

"Soccer 101!" she snapped. "If I go up, you move back. It doesn't take a genius!"

"You leave your mark and your position and it's somehow *my* fault?" Charlie asked. "Grow up!"

"It is your fault," Krista yelled. "You don't try to take the ball from someone on your own team!"

Krista noticed that their teammates were starting to gather around. Jamie put a hand on Charlie's shoulder to calm her. Charlie knocked it off.

Krista and Charlie were both soaking wet. The rain came down fast and hard. Charlie took a step closer to Krista, getting in her face.

"You can't stand that someone else would come in here and outshine the perfect, legendary Krista Brown. It makes you sick that I can do what you do, only better. You can't stand that I'm the one getting more attention than you—"

"You don't even know what you're talking about." Krista laughed. "You're insane."

"You couldn't believe that my new friends actually chose giving me attention over you, so you had to do the one thing that you knew would hurt me. You had to get Noah's attention—"

"Shut up," Krista interrupted, panicking. She couldn't let Charlie finish that sentence. She grabbed her arm.

"Get away from me," Charlie screeched. She pushed Krista, hard. Krista stumbled backward into Jen behind her.

In that moment, she was so angry at Charlie, she literally couldn't see straight. She lunged for her sister, and the referee intervened, keeping them apart.

A whistle blew, snapping Krista out of her rage. She looked up and took in the ref's expression. It was true horror—as though he didn't know whether to pull out a yellow card, a red card, or a restraining order.

Martie rushed over from the sidelines. "Krista! Charlie! Get off this field right now! You are both officially suspended from play."

Krista sat on the team bus with her head in her hands. She couldn't think of anything worse than being kicked off the field. Her parents had been in the stands, so many kids from Beachwood had driven out. . . . She felt sick to her stomach thinking of how she'd let them all down. She was absolutely humiliated.

Her parents had left to head back to Malibu, not wanting to suffer through the downpour if their girls weren't even playing. They'd wanted to take her home, along with Charlie, but according to the rules, neither one of them could leave until Martie released them.

Krista shook her head. The steady rain tapped on the bus's metal roof. All else was silent.

Then the crowd inside the Pomona arena roared. Krista strained to see the scoreboard through the rain-flecked bus window.

No! Madison had scored again. Beachwood was down by two. If they didn't win, they were out of states.

Just like that. All their hard work was down the drain.

Krista balled her hands into fists. *She* should be out there. *She* should be leading her team to victory. Instead, she was trapped on this stupid bus with her selfish sister.

She felt bottled up, like she was going to explode. She slammed her fists down on the seat in front of her and spun around to face Charlie, who was sitting in the last seat.

"They just scored again," Krista yelled as tears began streaming down her face. "How could you have done this?"

Charlie scowled and remained silent.

pretty
TOUGH

"We should be out there!" Krista pointed toward the lit-up field. "We had a chance. You—you ruined everything!"

Charlie jumped up. Now she was crying too. "No, *you* ruined everything!"

"Why? Because of Noah?" Krista cried. "Noah doesn't have anything to do with this."

"He has *everything* to do with it," Charlie screamed back.

Krista shook her head. "I didn't know you were even interested in Noah!"

Charlie glared at Krista, a look of complete disbelief on her face. "You still don't get it, do you?" she spat, using her hands to wipe the tears away. Krista had never seen Charlie cry this hard. "I'm *not* interested in Noah! I never *was* interested in Noah!"

"Then what the hell is this all about?" Krista yelled back.

Charlie's face turned purple, and for a moment, she could barely speak. She took a minute to collect herself.

"This isn't about some stupid boy or some stupid crush," she said slowly between breaths. "This was about me getting a life! This was about finding people who believed in me—supported me. This was about me standing in the spotlight for once—and then you came and stole it all away!"

Krista's jaw dropped open.

"For *one time*," Charlie added, *"this wasn't about you."*

Before Krista could respond, a huge flash of lightning lit up the sky. A second later, the thunder clapped so loudly she could feel the bus rumble.

Suddenly, everyone was streaming out of the arena, running toward the parking lot—the crowd, the players, the referees.

Krista's teammates, wet, muddy, and cold, piled onto the bus. None of them would speak to her, but Krista did gather that Beachwood had received the luckiest of breaks. The game was called due to weather. At least one good thing had happened—Beachwood was still in the tournament.

"You can come in now."

Charlie looked up from her spot on the floor outside Martie's hotel room door. Martie was standing there in the doorway without even a hint of a smile on her face.

Charlie got up slowly. Painfully. Her whole body ached.

As she walked past her coach, Charlie had no idea what was going to happen, but as far as she was concerned, Martie could just end it all here. This whole soccer experience had turned into one big fat disaster. And now, to top it off, the entire team was mad at her.

She could be sent home for all she cared—and maybe she *should* be. Martie would just be putting her out of her misery.

"Martie, I—" she began.

Martie held up a hand, stopping her cold. "No, Charlie. No. I don't want to hear your excuses. I told you to let me know if there was something going on. I told you to sort it out before the game."

"I know," Charlie insisted, "but you don't understand—"

"No, *you* don't understand," Martie interrupted. "I've been teaching you and coaching you for months. What have you even learned?"

Charlie was taken aback. "I—I've started every single game. You never sub me out for more than five minutes. I score the most goals of any player on the team! How can you say I haven't learned anything?"

Martie shook her head. "You haven't learned the most important thing. That this isn't a competition between you and your sister."

Charlie gave a bitter laugh. "Yeah, right. We were playing great before—"

She stopped herself before she could say any more.

"Before what?" Martie asked curiously.

"Just before."

Charlie might be angry with her sister, but she wasn't a rat. If Martie found out about Noah and Krista, it wasn't going to be because of her.

"You mean *before* . . . when you were getting all the glory and attention and Krista was sucking it up and letting you have it?" Martie asked.

Charlie frowned. "No, it wasn't like—"

"Or *before*, when the *Peanuts* theme was blaring for you and Krista applauded along with everyone else, trying to support you when you wouldn't give her the time of day?"

Charlie grimaced. "But she—"

"When are you going to realize that there's room in the spotlight for both of you? That there's enough of everything good to go around? It doesn't have to be just one of you or the other."

Charlie sat on the bed and placed her head in her hands. "You wouldn't understand."

Martie folded her arms across her chest. "Wouldn't I?"

"No," Charlie said. "You don't know what it's like. To have a perfect sister like Krista. Someone right next to you who is so pretty, so smart, so *everything* that no one even sees you. And when they do pay attention to you, they're only doing it because they want to get close to *her*."

Martie was quiet for a long time. Charlie felt like she might have upset her coach but didn't know why. Martie should be *happy* she didn't have a sister like Krista.

Finally, Martie spoke. "Did you ever read the book I gave you? *To Kill a Mockingbird*?"

Charlie blinked, confused. "What do you mean? I took the test. I got a B-plus—"

"I know, but you didn't finish the book, did you?"

"No," Charlie admitted. She sighed and stood up.

"Look, Martie, are you letting me back on the team or not?"

Martie shrugged. "Finish the book and I'll let you know."

Charlie gaped at her coach. "What? But I—I don't have it with me."

"Great. Even better." Martie opened her closet and fished around in her overnight bag.

"Take my copy," she said, handing an old, dog-eared paperback to Charlie. "I expect you to finish it before tomorrow's game."

Charlie stared at the book in her hands. "There's no way I'll be done with this by tomorrow night. And what does *To Kill a Mockingbird* have to do with soccer any-way?"

"Read it, Charlie. You won't play until you do." Martie opened the door to her room so that Charlie could walk through. "We're done here. Now it's up to you."

Charlie sat in the lobby, book in hand. She didn't see the point. What did some stupid book have to do with soccer or Krista or anything? And why was Martie making her read it? Either she should be playing in tomorrow's game or going home.

A cool burst of air blew into the hotel as the glass doors opened. It was Noah, returning from a soda run.

Charlie quickly looked down, not wanting to make

eye contact. She concentrated on ignoring him with every fiber of her being.

It didn't matter. He took a seat next to her on the couch.

"So . . ." he said awkwardly.

Charlie snorted. She supposed he hadn't known what else to say . . . but *that's* what he had come up with? *"So?"* Brilliant.

"You talked to Martie, right?" Noah asked.

"Don't worry," Charlie muttered. "I didn't say anything about your little secret with Krista."

"That's not why I'm asking," he said. "But thanks."

More silence. Charlie wasn't going to make it easy on him.

"Listen, Charlie," he continued, "whatever my relationship is with your sister, it doesn't have anything to do with how I feel about you."

Charlie squinted at her book, trying to appear like she was focusing on the words. "Uh-huh."

"I believe in you. I think you're the best player on that field. You play with your heart out there. If you'd just use your head a little more—look around, listen, not just when things are going well off the field, but every single time you set foot on that grass . . . If you do that, you'll be the one with colleges banging down your door trying to sign you. You can't let this stupid thing ruin all the hard work you've done all year—"

pretty
TOUGH

Charlie turned the other way. Noah stopped short.

"Whatever," he said, giving up. "If Martie's story about her sister didn't get through to you, my little pep talk probably isn't."

Charlie looked up, confused. "Martie and *her sister?* What're you talking about?"

Noah gave her a funny look. "The accident? And the settlement money?" Suddenly, he stopped. "Didn't she tell you . . . ?"

Charlie had absolutely no idea what he was talking about.

"Well, if she didn't tell you, I'm not sure I should." He studied her for a moment. "Oh, what the hell. It's important, and you need to hear it." He took a deep breath. "Martie had a sister who also went to Beachwood. They played here together. Martie went on to play, you know, for the National team. Her sister got a scholarship to UCLA and played there. Martie was out of the country, at a World Cup competition, when she got a call. Her sister had been in an accident—nothing to do with soccer—it was a drunk driver."

Charlie gasped. "Her sister . . ."

She couldn't even say it. It was too horrible.

"She died," Noah confirmed. "That's where the money came from. For the endowment. It was the settlement money from the lawsuit."

"Wait a minute," Charlie said slowly. "Martie's the

anonymous benefactor? She's the one who donated all the money to rebuild the program?"

Noah nodded. "Beachwood soccer was something that really mattered to Martie and Corrine. That was her sister's name, Corrine. She said it was what brought them together. Even if Martie was the better player, she always looked to Corrine on the field. She was still her big sister, Martie said."

Charlie sat stunned. She'd had *no* idea. She doubted any of the girls did.

For one brief, awful moment, Charlie thought about what she would do if anything happened to Krista.

"Does Krista know?" she asked Noah. "About Corrine?"

Noah shook his head. "Just you. Martie didn't want anyone to know, but . . . she told me she was going to tell you, so . . . I just thought . . ."

Charlie knew why Martie hadn't told her story. Because of what Charlie had said about not knowing what it was like to have a sister. She felt sick to her stomach, like the biggest jerk in the world.

She owed Martie a huge apology. "I'm sorry" wasn't even enough. She had to find another way. She realized she needed to start something she'd promised to finish.

"Could you excuse me?" Charlie asked Noah. "I have a lot of reading to do before our game tomorrow."

It was almost four in the morning when Krista felt a sensation that she hadn't in years. Her eyelids were being lifted up one by one.

"Are you awake?" a voice asked.

Krista opened her eyes. Charlie was sitting on her bed.

When they were little, every Saturday morning and every day in the summers, Charlie would rise early—way before Krista—and the rule from her parents was that Charlie couldn't wake her.

So instead, she would sneak into Krista's room and peel back her eyelids one at a time, asking that same question, "Are you awake?"

It always worked—even now.

Krista sat up and rubbed her eyes. "What?"

"I'm sorry. I know you're sleeping, but there's something—there's something I need to say," Charlie whispered.

"Can't it wait until morning?" Krista asked.

"No," Charlie insisted. "It can't."

Krista frowned and folded her arms across her chest. "Well, what is it?"

Charlie swallowed hard, then grew silent. She opened her mouth, closed it. Opened her mouth, closed it again.

Seconds ticked by. Krista sighed. Maybe her sister *was* psycho.

"This is ridiculous," she said. "I'm going back to sleep." She grabbed her covers and began to roll over.

"No, wait!" Charlie placed a hand on her shoulder.

Krista turned back and stared at her.

"I wanted to say something . . . about a book I just read," Charlie started over. "The book is called *To Kill a Mockingbird*. Martie lent me her copy earlier. There's a line in it that she underlined—she even put a star next to it in the margin. The line says: *Atticus told me to delete the adjectives and I'd have the facts*."

Krista scowled, genuinely puzzled. "Charlie, what is this? It's four in the morning!"

But Charlie plowed on. "I thought about what that meant and why that one line was so important. Then I thought about deleting the extra words between us—all the things we've said to each other that were hurtful or spiteful—things that didn't amount to anything—until I got to the facts. And when I thought of all the words I could and threw them all out, there was just one I couldn't let go of. *Sister.* Because that's what we are, and that's the fact."

"So?" Krista asked.

"So, maybe you've done things that hurt me or disappointed me. I know I've done things that hurt you. But I wanted to tell you—" Charlie swallowed. Her eyes grew shiny with tears. "I wanted to tell you that I'm sorry—for all of it."

Krista stared at her little sister. A lump formed in her throat. "Charlie, why are you saying all of this?"

pretty
TOUGH

"Because I realized something tonight: you're the reason I pushed myself so hard. You're the reason I discovered how much I love this team. I know we've fought, but without you, I wouldn't be here. Honestly, I don't know where I'd be."

"Charlie—" Krista started.

"I thought I wanted to be better than you," Charlie admitted, "but really, I just wanted to be more like you, So I'm hoping—I'm hoping that we can start over. I want us to be what we really are—deep down, beyond anything else. I want us to be sisters."

Krista gazed at her sister in amazement. "Oh, Charlie. You don't want to be like me. I think—I think I should be more like *you*. You're not afraid to speak your mind. You stand up to people. You know who you are, and you don't pretend to be something you're not. You're tough, you're fearless. And you're strong—you're so strong, Charlie."

She paused for a moment, the words stuck in her throat. "If it had been me with Regan that day in the cafeteria—if it had been me instead of you—you wouldn't have cared what anyone else thought. You would have defended me."

Charlie looked down at her hands.

"I let you down," Krista admitted, "but I promise you, it will never, ever happen again." She felt a single tear spill down her face.

Charlie looked up. Krista saw that she was crying

too. She grabbed her sister in her arms and squeezed. It was the first hug they'd shared in . . . Krista couldn't even remember how long.

"Kris?" Charlie whispered after a while.

"Yeah," she answered.

"Hug . . . too tight," Charlie gasped. "Can't breathe."

Krista laughed and let her sister go.

Charlie smiled back at her. "So," she said, "which one of us is going to tell Martie we're playing today?"

Krista shrugged. "I will. It seems like a big sister thing to do."

As Krista got up and slipped on her sweatshirt and grabbed her key off the dresser, Charlie made her way over to the bed to get some sleep. She climbed in next to Carla, who tapped her on the arm.

Charlie jumped, startled that Carla was awake.

"I'm proud of you, Charlie," she said.

Charlie snuggled down under the covers and smiled.

When Charlie woke up just a few hours later, she felt amazingly well rested, considering she'd had only a few hours sleep. Today was a clean slate. With the game yesterday being rained out, it was as if their tournament was actually beginning today. It was a rare opportunity for a second chance. Charlie was determined to make the most of it.

Sitting at breakfast between Carla and Jamie, she was

nervous. There was a free continental breakfast at the Marriott, and Charlie **had taken** advantage, eating both a bowl of Raisin Bran *and* a bagel. She couldn't help but laugh when she saw **Martie** grab two bananas.

Not all the girls were as happy to have Charlie and Krista back. Plenty of them stared and whispered, understandably hesitant. No one wanted a repeat of yesterday on the field. Charlie and Krista knew they had to make sure everyone knew that there wouldn't be.

The girls boarded the bus by nine o'clock and were at the field exactly twelve minutes later. The locker room buzzed with excitement as the team raced around, changing into their uniforms.

When the entire team gathered, Martie gave a pep talk.

"Okay, you guys," she said excitedly. "We get another chance today. Another chance to be warriors on that field. Whatever you do, don't let down and don't give up. Just relax and play like you've practiced. Don't let yourself get frazzled. Play with your head *and* your heart out there. Okay—hands in—"

"Wait," Charlie interrupted. "I—I mean, um—*we* have something we want to say."

Martie looked taken aback. Noah gave Krista an uneasy look.

Krista smiled reassuringly and stepped forward. "B-dub, we've been through a lot this season," she said. "So much that we're more than teammates. We're sisters. All of us."

"We overcame the odds and have already put Beach-wood soccer back on top," Charlie continued. "That's because of one person—one person who believed we could do it: Martie Reese. So Krista and I want to thank her for reminding us . . . how important our sisters are." She draped an arm around Krista's shoulders and squeezed.

Martie put a hand to her lips. Her eyebrows knit together, like she was trying to hold something in.

"That's how we have to go out there and play today." Krista picked up the thread. "As one unit—as sisters. If we listen to each other and treat each other with respect, there's no way we can lose."

Charlie saw a tear roll down Martie's cheek. She quickly wiped it away.

Martie walked across the locker room to Charlie and Krista. She put an arm around each of them.

"Girls, I want you to know I am proud of each and every one of you," she said. "Now let's go. Everyone. Hands in."

All the girls piled their hands in the center. This time when Krista put her hand in, Charlie made sure to put her hand right on top. Noah put his in last to finish out the pile. And together everyone chanted, "Let's go, B-dub. LET'S GO, BANANAS."

"Senior Krista Brown," the announcer boomed. Charlie clapped from the sidelines. The B-dub team had made it all the way to Saturday night, to the semifinal game.

The cheers for Krista were the loudest that Charlie had ever heard in her life. Fans tended to cheer most for the seniors because now, in play-offs, each game could be their last.

The announcer continued introducing the team. "Julie Theiser." "Zaida Wincelowicz." Charlie jumped in place to stay warm.

"Sophomore Charlie Brown." She sprinted onto the field. The cheers were deafening as she low-fived the other players. But when she jogged even with Krista, Krista gave her a hug.

"Good game," Krista said.

Charlie smiled. "You too." She took her place back at the end of the line beside Zaida.

"Carla Hernandez." Carla ran out to take her place. Once in line, Charlie saw Carla's mom and brother going crazy in the stands. Nate had offered to give them a ride out so they could see Carla play for the first time. Charlie knew Carla had been extremely nervous about what her mother would think. Charlie smiled. Mrs. Hernandez looked extremely proud.

On Mrs. Hernandez's left sat Bryan. He waved to her. She gave a little half wave back, trying hard to conceal her smile. In front of him were Pickle and Benji, who had driven up as well. The two of them were going crazy!

"Go, Charlie! Go, Carla!" they screamed in unison.

As the national anthem played and the lights shone down, Charlie took a deep breath and whispered, "Please let tonight be my lucky night."

Fifteen minutes later, as her body slid along the grass and dirt, Charlie knew luck was going to have nothing to do with this victory. Her foot tipped the ball and knocked it out-of-bounds, ending Andover's run for the goal.

"Nice try, Charlie." Martie clapped from the sidelines.

Andover headed the ball in and Darcy jumped up to grab it. No goal.

"Charlie!" Darcy yelled.

Charlie responded quickly. She went for the ball and was the first one to it. She cut back, avoiding an Andover defender, successfully dribbling around her.

"You got my back," Krista yelled as Charlie raced toward their eighteen, the other players descending on her.

"She's on, she's on!" Krista warned, letting Charlie know the player marking her was right on her heels.

Charlie shot the ball back to Krista, who knocked it to Jen. Jen quickly trapped it and gestured to Ruthie and Charlie to get open. Charlie cut in front of the Andover stopper and Jen passed the ball. Charlie jumped and kicked while still in the air, her shoe making contact with the ball. It was a beautiful shot, perfectly placed . . . the kind of goal that would be replayed again and again . . . except the Andover goalie caught it.

Charlie ran back toward Krista, who slapped her on the back.

"Good try," she said. Charlie nodded. She couldn't believe how great it felt to have her sister behind her, encouraging her. All this time she thought she had to succeed *despite* her sister; she never thought she could succeed *because* of her. Working with Krista was so much easier than working against her. And working with her because she *wanted* to was a totally different feeling.

When Beachwood got a corner kick a few minutes later, Jamie was called up to take it. Charlie knew Krista got nervous for corner kicks because everyone was crowded in. It felt like twenty players, ten from each team, going for the ball once it was put into play.

"Stay strong, Krista," Charlie shouted encouragingly, getting into her position in the middle of the pack. "We've got this." Her spot was right in the thick of things with Buffi, Ruthie, Heather, and Jen, who were heavily marked by the Andover defenders. They were all so close, so on top of each other, Charlie could feel the heat coming off the other players' bodies.

When Jamie booted the ball, Charlie watched in awe as Krista charged the goal line. Jumping up without hesitation, she beat the Andover defender to the ball and headed it right past their goalie and into the upper-right corner of the net. It was one of the hardest, coolest goals possible. The crowd erupted, and Krista was tackled by her teammates. It was the first goal of the night.

"You did it!" Charlie shrieked. "You did it! You took the header!"

Krista pumped her fists victoriously as her parents cheered wildly from the crowd. Even she seemed surprised.

Beachwood's celebratory mood, however, was cut short. Just a few minutes into the second half, Andover was inside Beachwood's eighteen. They managed to rebound the ball off the goalpost—right into the box. Darcy was devastated that she'd let a ball in. Carla took the blame, saying it was her fault. She'd lost track of her mark. Jamie gathered the defenders into a circle as Krista took the offense. Each had her own job to do on the field.

"You guys," Krista said. "We can do this. Let's go! Make their keeper work. We gotta take more shots."

Jamie brought the defenders over. "You guys, they can predict a lot of our plays. Let's switch it up more, okay? Don't be afraid to switch fields, switch positions. . . . Just make sure everyone is marked."

Krista nodded. Charlie looked between both of them. Krista and Jamie were great at strategy. They were going to get the ball up the field. Then it would be up to Charlie to put it into the net.

The next time the ball got down near Beachwood's net, Carla fought to get it out of there. She beat Andover to the ball and knocked it back to Erica. "Switch fields," Jamie yelled, and Erica booted a long ball clear across to Julie on the other side of the field, who quickly knocked it up to Karen.

Charlie felt her whole body tingling as she wiped the sweat out of her eyes. This was it. She knew what play was coming.

Karen passed to Krista, who dove in front of an Andover midfielder to get it. The midfielder tripped over Krista, ending up next to her on the ground. Carla grabbed the ball as Krista popped up.

"Move back," Carla yelled to Krista.

Krista moved back on defense, covering Carla's position and mark. As Carla ran upfield, Charlie moved to get open, elbowing an Andover defender out of her way.

As another defender bore down on Carla, she passed so she wouldn't lose the ball. Charlie sprinted to get the ball in time, colliding with an Andover defender but still managing to tap the ball to Ruthie. Ruthie knocked it to Carla, who had charged into Andover's eighteen. The crowd went wild, anticipating what was next.

Andover's stopper got to the ball first. She tried booting it out, but Charlie jumped to block her kick. WHACK! The ball pelted Charlie on the leg—so hard she was sure she would have a honeycomb imprint there permanently. It rebounded off her and Carla ran for it. She slid and knocked it right past the Andover goalie into the net.

The crowd erupted. Beachwood had scored!

Charlie jumped on Carla as their teammates crowded around them. Beachwood was now up two–one. Winning the game seemed not only possible, but likely . . .

. . . until a hand ball was called on Julie inside the eighteen.

"I didn't touch it!" Julie yelled to the ref. "I swear."

Martie protested the call. They were overruled.

"Andover," the ref indicated. "Shot on goal." The Beachwood section booed loudly.

"C'mon, guys," Krista encouraged. "Defense. No shoots, no scores."

The girls formed a human wall between Andover's kicker and Darcy. Charlie and Krista moved into the center.

Charlie hated the human wall. What could be scarier than standing directly in front of a ball that was about to be kicked right toward your face? It was difficult not to close your eyes or flinch or move . . . especially when a ball was hurling toward you.

And after all, her boobs were finally growing. Charlie chuckled to herself—all she needed now was for both of them to be flattened . . . or worse, just one of them!

The Andover player ran at the ball. She kicked!

The ball sailed high over Charlie's head. Andover had managed to avoid the wall completely. Inside the goal,

pretty
TOUGH

Darcy dove, but the ball whizzed past her. It hit the back of the net. They'd scored.

"Crap," Charlie said, a little too loudly.

"Good try, Darce," Krista encouraged.

With the game tied up two–two and one minute to go, it looked like the game would go into sudden death overtime, where the first team to score would win. Charlie ran hard in the last minute, desperate to avoid sudden death. She got one shot on goal, but it was rushed. It bounced off the post.

The whistle blew. Sudden death.

Sudden death was as scary as it sounded. One goal and the game was over.

And now, most of the girls were exhausted from playing a full game. Somehow, they'd have to stay strong.

Martie subbed Karen in for Heather and tried to sub Zaida in for Charlie, but Charlie insisted she was fine. She wasn't coming out of the game now. Zaida went in for Ruthie instead.

Beachwood played amazingly well—the ball barely made it down to their side of the field. They took at least four shots on goal—two attempted by Charlie—but the Andover goalie was a maniac. She caught balls no human being should have been able to get her hands on. Beachwood was shut out. At the end of sudden death, no one had scored. Which meant one thing—

"A shoot-out?" Charlie said in disbelief.

They hadn't had a shoot-out all season. She couldn't believe the irony. Here she and Krista had been struggling all year long to become teammates, and now their victory was going to come down to something that couldn't be more individual.

It would be kicker versus goalie on the field alone, under the glaring spotlight. And Noah had worked out the lineup. Jamie, Jen, Carla, Charlie, and Krista.

The shoot-out started with five players from each side shooting at goal one at a time. Whichever team scored the most during the shoot-out would win.

The goalie had to guess which side of the net the kicker would aim for—and she could only jump in one direction. If she jumped to the wrong side, there was no time to correct and go the other way. The pressure was enormous.

An Andover kicker went first, and Darcy chose to dive right. Lucky for her, so did the kicker. Darcy stopped the ball. On the Beachwood bench, the team went crazy.

Jamie was up first for B-dub. She took a deep breath. She was known for being a great kicker. She planned to boot the ball into the left-bottom corner. She ran, kicked—and somehow overshot. The ball skimmed the post and rebounded off it. Their goalie didn't have to do a thing to deflect it.

Jamie kicked the dirt in frustration. As she headed for

pretty
TOUGH

the bench, the other girls patted her on the back, comforting her. She sat down and buried her head in her hands.

Another Andover kicker took a shot. This time, Darcy wasn't so lucky. She jumped right again, but the kicker had faked and placed the ball to the left. It sailed past Darcy into the net. Andover was up one–nothing.

Jen was next. She took a powerful shot, but their goalie dove and caught it. Jen looked near tears as she joined Jamie on the bench. Krista and Charlie exchanged a nervous look. Beachwood still had zero to Andover's one.

Andover was up again and took a shot that Darcy caught easily.

Carla jumped up and down nervously. She was next.

"Come on, Carla," Krista encouraged.

Carla took a deep breath and approached the ball. BAM! She nailed it—right into the back of the net. Cheers exploded, her mom's the loudest of all. Carla beamed and gave her mother the tiniest of waves.

The score was now one–one.

Andover's next kicker knocked the ball into the corner, so close to the post that Darcy actually collided with it when she jumped. She blocked the shot but collapsed onto the ground. Medics rushed onto the field to help her.

A few minutes later Zaida, the second-string goalie, nervously replaced her.

If Beachwood was going to win, either Krista or

Charlie was going to have to make her goal, and Zaida couldn't let Andover score another.

Charlie was up next. All eyes were on her. In that moment, it was as if her entire year flashed before her eyes— Martie finding her surfing on the beach, the pickup game in Carla's neighborhood, Carla showing up in the Town Car, hell week and hell month and seeing her name on the list for the team, dancing with Bryan, that great goal she'd scored against Curtis, sitting with her father talking about soccer plays, getting a B-plus, laughing with Carla and Pickle so hard that her sides hurt, and peeling back Krista's eyelids.

It had all added up to this moment.

She took a deep breath, trying to calm the butterflies. She had to make it. She had to score. If she didn't, their season would be over. She'd worked too hard for it to end this way—with her losing the game for her team. Besides, she had two more years to play, but if they lost, this would be Krista's last game.

It had to be a win—for Krista.

As if in slow motion, Charlie willed herself to move. Her foot connected with the ball.

Boom! The ball sailed up and arced gracefully toward the net.

Charlie watched the Andover goalie dive . . . and catch it with both hands.

Charlie fell to her knees. She couldn't believe it. She hadn't scored. It was her moment and she blew it. All this season, she had been Beachwood's top scorer and now, when it mattered most, she'd blown it.

She took a seat on the bench and buried her head in her hands. She could feel the encouraging pats of her teammates on her back, but it didn't help. Nothing did. She'd failed. She'd let everyone down.

She heard more cheers around her, which meant Zaida had deflected Andover's final shot. Krista was the last to go. Only she could win the game for Beachwood.

Charlie couldn't watch. She closed her eyes tightly. She folded her hands together and touched her fingertips to her lips. She'd never been one to pray, but now all she could think was, *Please, please, please . . .*

She imagined only Krista and the Andover goalie left on the field. Charlie held her breath and waited.

BAM! She heard Krista's foot connect with the ball. Charlie looked up. She saw Krista on her knees, on the ground, looking up at the sky.

Oh no, thought Charlie. *No!*

But suddenly, her teammates were pushing into her, everyone trampling past everyone else to get out on the field. They were laughing and cheering and screaming. . . .

Charlie looked at the Andover bench. The girls were crying. It could only mean one thing.

They'd won!

Charlie raced past everyone, jumping over the pile of girls onto her sister.

"We won!" she screamed "We won!"

Martie and Noah joined the pile. Everyone was laughing and crying and waving to the adoring crowd. Charlie rolled out of the pile, still on her back, and looked up at the night sky. All she could see were the bright lights that shone down on them.

As parents and friends made their way onto the field to congratulate the winning team, the girls hoisted Krista onto their shoulders. Charlie looked up from her spot on the ground. The lights shone brightly down on Krista.

Charlie watched as if she was seeing a scene from a movie, not something that was actually happening.

Everything seemed to be in slow motion. Krista smiled and laughed and tried not to fall off Jamie and Zaida's shoulders. She gave a huge wave to all the fans. Charlie felt a wave of pride. This wasn't just Krista's moment. It was hers too. It was all of theirs. That's what she finally understood.

After the game, once most of the people had left and parents were waiting by their cars, the girls were gathering their belongings from the sidelines.

Charlie approached Bryan.

"Thanks for coming all the way out to watch," she said shyly. "Krista's great, huh?"

Bryan nodded. "You're great too."

Charlie blushed. Suddenly, Krista called to her.

"Hey, Charlie! A bunch of the Beachwood boys got a

suite at the Marriott. I think they're having a party for us. . . . Martie said we could go if we didn't stay out late."

Charlie remembered her fantasy—the one where Krista invited her to a party, wanted to hang out with her, asked her to come as if she belonged.

Now it was actually happening.

"Come on, Charlie," Krista called. "The bus is leaving."

Charlie turned back to Bryan. "You should come too," she said, hardly believing the bold words were coming out of her mouth.

He grinned. "Thanks. I'll see you there."

Charlie said good-bye and made her way to the bus in the parking lot.

As she took a seat, she couldn't wipe the smile off her face. This was what she'd always dreamed of, and now it was real.

It was as if it was all supposed to happen this way. All the ups and downs, all the fights and struggles . . . it somehow made the victory even sweeter.

Charlie might have wished things were a *little* different. Like, she wouldn't have minded making that last goal or having a name like Britney or Ashley.

But really, when all was said and done, who was Charlie Brown to argue with destiny?

acknowledgments

Thanks go to the many individuals who helped make this book a reality. First, to Jane Schonberger and George Morency whose lives are committed to empowering young women through sports. Thanks also to Carole Rosen and to Andy Barzvi and Jennifer Joel of ICM who were early supporters of Pretty Tough and extremely helpful in bringing the book to fruition. Editor extraordinaire Kristen Petit provided insightful notes, support and guidance along the way and Coach Stacy provided access to the high school soccer field as well as a glimpse into the hearts and minds of female athletes.

Thank you also to the 418+1 girls—jen, jamie, erica, buffi, fran, ruth, heather, julie, karen, and elizabeth—who I couldn't have written this without. And thanks to Nate and most importantly, my parents, Bob and Mary, and my sister, Kate. L.T

Pretty Tough is . . . getting up early for practice and staying late to finish a game. It's the way you think, the way you talk, the way you act, and the way you walk. It's an attitude. It's a motto for those who can see it through. It's the way you play and the work you do. It's never backing down. It's never letting up. Pretty Tough is busting stereotypes, reaching new dimensions, and pushing limits for the love of the game.